Jeff Talarigo

THE GINSENG HUNTER

Jeff Talarigo won the Academy of Arts and Letters Rosenthal Foundation Award for his widely acclaimed first novel, *The Pearl Diver*. After living in Japan for almost fourteen years, he moved back to the United States in 2006 with his wife and son. He was awarded a fellowship at the New York Public Library's Dorothy and Lewis B. Cullman Center for Scholars and Writers. *The Ginseng Hunter* is his second novel.

www.jefftalarigo.com

Also by Jeff Talarigo

The Pearl Diver

THE GINSENG HUNTER

ANCHOR BOOKS
A DIVISION OF RANDOM HOUSE, INC.
NEW YORK

ANCHOR BOOKS
A DIVISION OF RANDOM HOUSE, INC.
NEW YORK

THE GINSENG HUNTER

A NOVEL

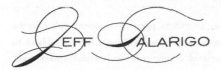

JEFF TALARIGO

FIRST ANCHOR BOOKS EDITION, APRIL 2009

Copyright © 2008 by Jeff Talarigo

All rights reserved. Published in the United States by Anchor Books,
a division of Random House, Inc., New York, and in Canada by Random House of
Canada Limited, Toronto. Originally published in hardcover in the United States
by Nan A. Talese, a division of Random House, Inc., New York, in 2008.

Anchor Books and colophon are registered trademarks of Random House, Inc.

The Library of Congress has cataloged the Nan A. Talese edition as follows:
Talarigo, Jeff.
The ginseng hunter / Jeff Talarigo.—1st ed.
p. cm.
1. Korea (North)—Fiction. I. Title.
PS3620.A525G56 2007
813'.6—dc22   2007011395

Anchor ISBN: 978-0-307-27523-3

Book design by Terry Karydes

www.anchorbooks.com

Printed in the United States of America
10   9   8   7   6

For those who have made it across,
And for those who haven't

And for my family of women,
And for Aya and Bella, so much a part of it

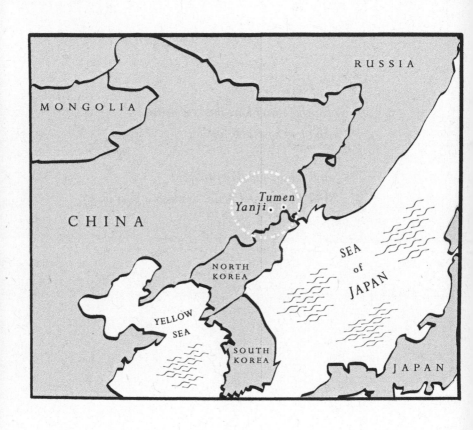

"But we all have moments when we must listen in tears to the silence of the swarming path inside ourselves."

—Kim Myong-In

THE GINSENG HUNTER

THE RIVER begins in a single country, and then crosses into another.

From the North Korean mountain range of Hamgyong and the Chinese range of Nangang, small rivers and streams feed into the Tumen River, and like the many rivers that begin deep in the mountains, the Tumen too is erratic, running head-high or shin-low, half a mile wide or fifty yards narrow, depending on the season.

It is a restless river, quickly leaving behind the pumice-capped mountains, running rough from its humble roots, and sometimes during a spring thaw, pounding over any flora that may be in its way. Ash and larch and white birch, a family of pines—Korean, white, sand.

In spring, for much of the morning, the mountains to the east deprive the river of the sun and allow it only a few hours of direct light before the mountains to the west steal it for the rest of the day. By late April the river remains frozen, shedding winter later than its surrounding landscape, this rugged frontier in the valley of the border region.

Along the Chinese border, in this first spring of the new century, a ginseng hunter stands along the river and watches it. That the river is frozen doesn't matter, perhaps it is best, for this is how it was last spring, when the whole of this valley began to change to a place he no longer recognizes.

THE OLD CENTURY'S FINAL SPRING

HIGH UP in the coniferous forest, the redwoods, with bodies as straight as a neck of ginseng, look down on me; their fragile, pale green leaves bow from stubby arms. I am humbled. This early morning, the first week of hunting season, is the same as all the other mornings. Only among the giant redwoods, some five thousand feet above my farm, am I able to push aside the worries that accompany me up from the valley below.

I slow to a hunting pace, sometimes covering less than one hundred yards in an hour. If I concentrate too hard on looking for the root, I may miss its presence one step away; however, if I allow my thoughts to disperse, like seeds of a dandelion in a soft breeze, the root will call out to me.

Moving along the path, I tread more cautiously for I know that under the forest floor the wars are fierce. What is seen on top may be serene, but beneath there is a battle for survival going on among the roots and weeds, all fighting over water and iron and copper and calcium and magnesium. Day after day. Bloodroot and jewel weed, galax and hepatica, ginger and wild yam. Ginseng must compete with all of them. It is this constant tension that gives the ginseng root its gnarled appearance—the wrinkles speaking of character more than of age. It is for this reason that every mature root I find is a celebration, a sign of survival.

This is my religion: everything I take from nature must be given back, to continue the cycle of life. In the coniferous forest, the root draws energy from both the sky and the earth. Only when man ingests the ginseng root is the cycle complete.

I stop in the middle of the path, and from a half-dozen steps away I can see a plant. A foot high, it is young, less than ten years old, but more than the seven years needed to reach maturity. Finding the root leaves me as excited as when I was a boy. My routine has remained unchanged: study the plant; review how best to approach it; estimate the angle and width of the circle I must make around it in order to begin digging; and unknot a red cloth from my belt. All the while, I keep an eye on the root as if it may dart away at any moment. Then I push a small stick into the ground, near the root, and mark it with the cloth.

Sprinkling water near the plant, I knead the ground with my palms, pausing to feel its energy. The root of a mature plant stretches more than a foot in length. The leaves, with soft hair on the front, are smooth on the back. I clip them, taking care not to break the neck of the root; as with man, a broken neck spells doom. I remove the spade from my cloth sack and peer closely at the root, inches from it, and then begin to draw a circle with the spade, two feet in circumference. With each spadeful of soil, I slowly expose the head of the root, which lies at a forty-five degree angle.

Now, as I close in on the legs of the ginseng, I put aside the small shovel and begin using only my hands. The dirt is deep and porous, the kind that permits the rain to pass. Two legs take shape as I pinch away more soil from them, exposing the beard, those long hairy rootlets at the leg's end. I pause. The beard is the most delicate part of the root, and even the slightest damage to it makes the root nearly impossible to sell. My hands are calm; the rest of my body is a blizzard. Taking a deep breath, I begin to clear away the soil that surrounds the beard. I work without hurry, and from time to time, with a gentle pull on the head, I test to see where the rootlets still grasp the earth. I fall into a steady rhythm, back and forth, removing the soil and tugging the root, until at last the beard is free. I lift and examine the whole root as a fisherman might do with his catch: by the head, holding it out, turning, checking it from top to bottom. It has the strong characteristics of wild ginseng: the nice bowed legs with the long beard branching out from them; the head with strong concentric wrinkles; the beautiful long neck. Tanned by the soil, the root will be a light yellow after rinsing.

Although it is still early, there will be no more hunting today. My father taught me never to be greedy with nature, never to take more than a single root in a day. In the cloth sack, I carry the root on my right shoulder—careful not to let it collide with the backpack on my left, which holds my tools and food and water for the day—and start down the mountain. My breathing is choppy, coming in gasps. I rest often. These early days of spring, after the long winter, my body and mind are not yet ready for the hunting season. With each passing year my mind seems to stay a few more paces ahead of my body.

I hear a stream and seek it out. I give the root a quick rinse in the current, then place it in the sack, which sops

7

up the excess water. Twice I drink from the stream, sending knives of cold through my teeth. I hang the sack on the branch of a tree, sit on a rock, and begin to eat slowly, taking the time to taste the potato cakes, pickled cabbage, and garlic cucumbers. The weather is near perfect, a little warm for early May. I open my cotton jacket and still am comfortable.

Today the hunting has been good. Although the root is not a great one, it is a good one. I know that I must find better roots to get me through the next winter, but that is in the future.

The forest is alive and the stream sounds as it did four decades ago, when I was a young boy. I eat another piece of dried ginseng, bundle my jacket into a pillow, and place it on the ground. Soon I am once again ten years old in the spring of 1960, when both the sparrows and the ginseng are plentiful.

I linger at the base of a thousand-year-old grandfather redwood, with roots splayed like giant toes. Surrounded by its ancestors—juniper, fir, cedar—it is the redwood I love; its thumb-sized cones will appear soon—cones that will drop months later and make the mountain's floor as slippery as the winter Tumen, but supply a soft and warm bed when you fall.

My father and uncle have left me here. I am alone for

the first time to hunt. Scraps of red cloth, for marking the places where I find ginseng, dangle from my pockets.

I repeat my favorite names for the root. Five Fingers. Tarter Root. Red Berry. Heaven Ginseng. Earth Ginseng. Emperor's Ginseng. By the time I hear the frost melting from the trees, signaling for me to start back, I have already used three pieces of red cloth.

Both my father and uncle are leaning against the ancient redwood, grinning at me; they have already finished their lunches. Only later do I learn that they have been sitting there for much of the morning, taking the day off.

"How is our hunter?"

I say nothing, holding up the remaining pieces of cloth. They flash me looks of surprise and exchange a knowing laugh, remembering what it's like to be fooled, understanding the way those memories—like an aged ginseng root—become less bitter and a little sweeter with time.

"Hurry and eat so we can uproot your treasures. We found nothing, not a single root."

The food doesn't go down easily. The lump of excitement makes swallowing difficult. I eat half and put what's left into a knapsack.

The two men are following me and soon we come upon the first red marker. All of us lean closer to the plant. I wait for words of praise. The longer the silence, the more uncomfortable I grow. I want to look at my father and uncle, but can't coax my head into doing so. Instead of words, it is the hands of my uncle that seem to speak. Taking hold of the five-leafed plant, he separates the leaves—three in his left hand, the other two in his right—and indicates where the leaves are attached.

"This is spikenard," my uncle tells me. "See how its five leaves are attached at two points? The ginseng's leaves are attached only at one. They are relatives, like you and I."

I feel as if I have been cheated; they never told me about this. While still holding the leaves, my uncle asks:

"Did you get close to the plant?"

"I guess not close enough."

"It's okay, we have all made the same mistake in the beginning," my father says.

"Why didn't you teach me?"

"Because now you will remember the lesson much better. Let's go and check the other two plants you found."

"Why? I made the same mistake with them."

"Maybe you didn't."

"I know I did."

"Still, we must retrieve the flags."

"I want to go by myself."

"That's fine. We will wait for you here."

"No, go home."

But my father doesn't leave the mountain; he is still sitting under the redwood when I return. He takes one of the red cloths and leads me away from the path that would take us down the mountain.

"I thought we would do some hunting together. We still have several hours before the sun sets."

I say nothing, still embarrassed by my failure. We walk for a long time before my father talks.

"You must step softly; imagine you are hunting an animal, not a plant."

"But the plants can't hear."

"No, they can't. There are many hints, though, many sounds that tell a person that a plant, ginseng or otherwise, is nearby."

I concentrate on walking lightly. Suddenly my father grabs me by the shoulder and points upward. I look, but my father wants me to listen instead; his grip is strong, without impatience.

The trees are swaying slightly in the wind, and at first this is the only sound—until I hear a bird. My father's hand tightens and he points off to the left. Again, the bird. Then it is gone and the chants of the murmuring trees become louder once more.

"That was a sparrow. Did you notice its voice?"

"Yes," I answer hesitantly. I'm not sure what the voice means.

"This is the best time to hunt ginseng, just after its tiny yellow flowers give way to the red berries on the plant. When the sparrows eat the berries their high-pitched calls become throatier. When you hear this throaty call, you only have to follow where it comes from and it will lead you to the plant. My grandfather taught me this secret."

While he talks, my father continues pointing to the left and we walk in that direction. We go a mere fifty yards when I spot the red-berried plant. I glance at my father, who is looking at me. For the first time in my life I experience the thrill of finding a root, but the feeling is quickly tempered.

"Take out your spade," my father urges.

Nervously, I open my knapsack and remove the spade, made of bone—according to superstition, ginseng is afraid of metal. It was better this morning with only the trees looking over my shoulder. Now, my father is also watching.

"Is the plant mature enough?"

"Yes," I answer.

"How can you tell?"

"It is more than a foot high and it has five leaves. Younger plants are shorter and have only three or four leaves."

Seeing my father smile, I feel more confident that I can extract the root without damaging it.

"Remember, always overestimate the length of the legs and beard. Sometimes a young root stretches out farther than you think."

I am aware of my father's presence as I work, but now I understand what he says about concentrating so hard that you don't notice anything else around you.

"You're doing fine, but move more in a circular direction. There should be no angles while you are digging around the root. Always in a circle to avoid any unexpected twists and bends of the ginseng legs."

My arms are not tired but maintaining my focus is becoming more difficult. I hear fragments of sentences: "yellow-whitish color . . . ovoid-shaped berries . . . the pearly spots on the beard."

When I finally have the root in hand, my father's words become complete sentences again.

"How old is the root?"

I examine the neck and, as I was taught, count the scars that have been left behind each autumn when the stem falls away from the neck, one scar per year; much like determining the age of a tree by its rings.

"Eight years old."

"That is a very good root to find as your first. It is nearly as old as you. Tonight, when we arrive home, we will store it in a glass jar filled with alcohol. A hunter never sells his first root."

After rinsing the root in a stream, we retrace our steps. My father has given me the root to carry. What I have yet to learn is that this first time I hunt the root by the sparrow's call will also be the last.

A few days later my father, mother, uncle, and I leave the house in the early morning carrying not the tools of hunters, but those of cooks.

Although it is the rainy season it isn't raining. My uncle's shoulders seem to slope with certain sadness, and my father's breath seems to be without its usual smell of steamed millet. I am not sure why everything feels so burdened this morning, only that it has something to do with the birds.

The night before, while lying on the heated brick *kang*, I heard my father speaking of Chairman Mao's orders to eliminate the sparrows, which were eating the grain before it could take root. "The villagers and farmers are to be mobilized," said my father. "Too many times we are being used to try and solve the nation's problems." I fell asleep and didn't hear my father explain the reason for the pots and pans, the ones I am carrying now for everyone to see.

I have two fry pans, my father three pots, my mother several lids, my uncle a couple of small woks. I try to carry both pans in the same hand. This, for some reason, makes me feel less self-conscious. But they make a lot of noise, smacking together, and under my uncle's silent glare, I move one of the pans to my left hand.

Every few minutes I have to switch the pans from hand to hand, since one is twice as heavy as the other. We are halfway to the village of Sanhe before we see another person; a girl, a few years older than I, is coming toward us. Immediately I want to hide my pans in the brush, even though she too is carrying some pots. But that makes sense: she is a girl. Little by little we spot more villagers, and they seem in better spirits than my family. Maybe if it rained, we could all go home. I could rid myself of these stupid pans and gather my tools and go out hunting. I look forward to the rain, which makes the red berries on the older plants shine.

But there will be no rain on this day. Throughout the countryside, on the south end of the village, people are converging on the paths, some stopping and joining those in the fields, while my family moves on. The weight of the pans pulls at my arms. I begin to wonder if it is possible for arms to stretch so much that they drag on the ground. We are about half a mile on the other side of Sanhe when finally we stop. I drop the pans; one of them clanks when it strikes a rock. Neither my uncle nor father turns my way, but I can feel their reproach.

"Pick up the pans." I hear my father's tobacco-scratchy voice.

All over the fields we see sparrows pecking at seeds and grain. When a deafening clang-clang-clanging of pots and pans engulfs the valley, the frightened birds spring from the ground, as do I. The sparrows are in the air, clouds of them, and my father is screaming.

"Pound the pans!"

I hit the two blackened bottoms together. The jolt of the pans reverberates up and down my arms, all the way to my teeth, aftershock after aftershock, so many of them that I think my teeth will shatter. Everyone is doing the same thing; hundreds of villagers banging pots and pans and tin cans and metal bars, anything to scare the sparrows, to keep their wings flapping. Faster, faster the pots and pans. Flapping, flapping the wings. The noise of each drowns out the other.

My arms are tired. Why don't the sparrows, with their flapping wings, fly away? What I couldn't know is that throughout the valley, the province, and the country, there are farmers and villagers, a continuous chain of people banging pots and pans like we are, all following Chairman Mao's orders so that if the sparrows were to fly away, they would not find a quiet place to land and rest.

The birds hover over the fields in unmoving clouds, exhausted, until they cannot move their wings any longer; they begin to drop, enormous black rain drops bouncing, thudding off the fields. The clouds of birds begin to shrink and gradually the sky reappears.

People begin running to the fallen birds; there are not only sparrows but other types of birds as well. They wring the birds' necks and leave them to blacken the fields everywhere.

"Let's go, son, we have done more than enough."

My father takes the two pans from me, tucks one under each arm, and we head back toward home.

Over the following days, people bring sacks filled with beaks to the local administrators, and for their efforts they are given buttons with the face of Chairman Mao. My father tells me that if I ever came home with a Mao button, although rare in those days, he would break my legs and leave me out among the hills of sparrows. Nearly forty years will go by before I, as a middle-aged man, will see hills as sad as these.

The summer that the sparrows were killed, the harvest was abundant; however, my father warned us that when nature is interrupted it will seek revenge. Nature's response came the following summer.

I am awoken by loud pinging outside the house. I think a storm must be shoving its way through the valley, the wind is splattering large drops of rain against the shutters. But then I realize that the rainy season has already passed. The sound only grows louder and more persistent, the wind hums rather than howls; and soon my entire family is awake.

My mother cautiously opens the shutters, and before

she can snap them shut again, the house is buzzing with locusts. Once again, we must use the tools of the kitchen
against nature. My father's words are prophetic: "Without
the sparrows to eat them, the locusts will thrive."

We swing the fry pans at the squall of locusts, and by the
time we have killed most of them, we are all drenched in
sweat; we can't open a shutter or door to invite in a breeze.

"Fill the backpacks," my father tells my mother.

"How much food do you need?"

"As much as we can carry."

My mother looks at my father.

"You are coming with us," he says.

The backpacks, crammed with food and hunting tools,
wait by the door. My family listens for the roar of the locusts to die down before we step out into the night, our
heads covered by woks. The noise of the locusts under our
feet makes it sound like we're walking through the fallen
autumn leaves.

Somewhere between fear and fascination I am trapped;
I have always liked insects, but now there are too many of
them. Maybe if it was daylight and I could see them, I
wouldn't feel as if they were suffocating me. There is a
strange deep blackness all through the valley, different
from the nights when bloated clouds are close to the
ground and block the stars. Maybe it is the noise that
makes the darkness so different. It isn't until we are well
up in the mountains that, through a break in the trees, I see
that the stars are out.

My mother's presence makes the climb unlike earlier
ones. I notice that my father and uncle act differently. Their

speech seems more restrained; stepping carefully around words, they do not resort to their usual banter—jokes I rarely understand, but still laugh at. Nor do I hear any reference to our trips to Yanji, which would also make my father and uncle snicker. Later, when the three of us are out hunting, they are just as quiet, as if they are worried that their voices might carry from one tree to another, all the way back to my mother.

Some days, despite my stubborn protests, my father orders me to stay at the camp and help my mother. Secretly, I cherish these times alone with her.

She tells me that when she was my age, her father worked for the Japanese army in the highest reaches of this forest, chopping down some of the oldest trees. So many trees were cut down that the rays of the sun began penetrating the woods all the way to the forest floor. As I look around, I can't imagine the place any darker during the day.

"When I was a girl, it was nearly always night in this forest, not like it is now when the sun and moon keep the time. I would come up here with my father and mother and sit more than a mile from where they were working. My father would shimmy high into the trees while my mother would wait at a safe distance. From where I was sitting I could hear the trees moan, a slow moan, as they began their long fall to the ground. This crying was one of the saddest things I have ever heard. Even sadder, for me, was their vibration as they crashed heavily to the earth. Afterward my mother would run over to the trees and saw them into pieces. I don't know if it is true, but I heard that my parents were killed by a tree; my father was clinging to the top of the giant cedar when it broke unexpectedly and plunged in the wrong direction, crushing my mother beneath it. I wasn't there, but I know that the both of them died on the same day and my aunt raised me."

I watch my mother cleaning potatoes in the stream; I have never heard this story. But before I can think of anything to say, she asks me to help her with the vegetables.

"What do you think you are doing, washing a stone?"

I pull the potato from the stream and turn to my mother, whose cotton trousers are wet to the thigh. She takes the potato away from me.

"A potato is no different than burdock root or ginseng—or a child, for that matter. You need a balance of toughness and tenderness; treat it with equal consideration. All are gifts from nature."

My mother scrubs the potato's skin with her raspberry-red knuckles, using enough strength to clean it. At the camp, after assembling a triangle of wood and starting a fire, she takes the potatoes, eases them into the boiling water, so gently that she risks scalding her fingers. A very different style from that of my father, who would toss the potatoes into the water with so little care that if I were standing too close I would get splashed and burned.

My father's lessons were always direct and straight to the point, whereas my mother's lessons were meant to be savored.

19

Once I was playing in the harvest-scarred garden when my mother put down her rake and told me to come into the shed with her. She then examined the paint brushes lying on the shelf, picking the smallest of them.

"Choose two colors from your uncle's paints."

"He told me never to touch them."

"Don't worry. It's okay. Take any two colors that you want and bring them outside. Make sure they are bright colors."

After selecting a light blue and a bright red, I went out to the garden and found my mother on her knees, her face close to the soil.

"What are you looking for?"

"I'm looking at the ants. There are so many of them and they are large. What colors did you pick?"

"Blue and red." I held them out for her to see.

"Those are perfect colors."

My mother handed me the brush.

"Try to find two of the largest ants that you can and paint the tops of them, each a different color. When you are finished, rinse the brush and put the paints and the brush back in the shed. I need to return to the raking."

I looked at the ants crawling around: some were hauling food, others had bits of leaves and grass, still others had nothing. I found a large ant that wasn't carrying anything and picked it up, dabbed it with the light blue paint, and put it back in the garden. It was a while before I could find another ant to paint with the red color that was as large and not carrying anything.

As my mother had instructed, I cleaned and dried the

brush and returned the paints to their proper places on the shelf. Back in the garden, I searched for the painted ants, but could not find them. With my hands, I dug and dug, deep into the soil, turning over the fallen leaves, but I still didn't see them. I took handfuls of dirt and wanted to throw them out of frustration.

"I can't find the ants I painted," I told my mother later.

"Nature has its own pace, which you must respect."

The following morning my mother's firmness still stung. My father and uncle had already left the house, and I hesitated before going to the *kang* and joining her under the blanket. But the morning was cold and so I ran from my bed to the *kang*. She lifted the blanket. I could feel the warmth from her body and from the heated brick platform floor. My ears were cold, and my mother placed her warm hands on top of them until they had warmed back up.

The pace of nature, which my mother spoke of, was never more evident than when we finally returned to the valley from the forest in the late summer of 1961. The locusts had destroyed that year's harvest. By winter, famine ravaged the entire country and my mother weakened. She was the first in my family to die of starvation. One season later my uncle, too, succumbed to exhaustion and died—along with 30 million others all over China. The first of Chairman Mao's many experiments had failed.

Before my mother died, my father and I would often

talk. Like the first time I found the root, he would calmly explain the techniques of hunting, teach me the various species of trees and undergrowth, and show me the way through the forest, pointing out which plants were edible and which were not. The greater the distance between us and the valley, the more we would have to discuss. But in time, as I became a better hunter, there became less for us to talk about; our shared love for nature left us with little to say.

After my mother and uncle were gone, the silence between my father and me grew. It was an easy quiet, one without tension. But I missed my mother; I missed coming home at the end of a day of hunting to her voice, which would fill the room.

My father lived nearly a decade longer than my mother and uncle, but I believe that he began to die the summer we killed the sparrows. My father had been a man of clear-cut routines who stubbornly clinged to them. Overnight his routines were stopped, his beliefs altered.

From the day that we walked home past the mountains of sparrows, my father hauled gloom with him for the remainder of his life, gloom that would permeate my solitude like the feel of the redwood's bark on my skin.

From more than a mile away, I hear the gabbling ducks gathering around my shed. I take the mountain trail. Although the route is longer and I am tired, I enjoy coming upon the ducks from the direction of the forest rather than from the river's. The ducks are the surest sign that hunting season has arrived; for as long as I can remember, they have faithfully returned to my farm every year.

The ducks' noises grow louder as I wind my way through the woods. The thought of their welcoming sight has renewed my energy, and my pace increases. At the point where the path bends around my three-acre farm I can see them strutting around. I admire their ability to keep so clean as they traipse around the muddy yard. I glance down, amused at my own mud-spattered boots and pants.

I trample through the wet weeds. One duck, then another, then all the ducks notice me. Unlike the ginseng plants, they are not shy and seem as happy to see me as I am them.

While removing my boots, I leave the door of my house open and a duck rushes past me into the front of my three rooms, meandering around, butting the dead stove with its bill, butting it again and again, before turning into another room.

I go to the back and open the storage closet, shuffle through cans and sacks and jars until I find the corn mixture, which I heap onto a tin pan. Leading the ducks around the house to the front of the shed, I toss the grain all over the ground. The ducks swarm, jostle one another, to claim their food.

Inside the house I clean the tools from the light day of work. Carefully swishing the ginseng root in a bucket of water, I watch the soil release itself and leave behind only enough dirt to emphasize the rings and let the buyer know the kind of soil in which it has grown. I place the root on the wooden drying rack with those from the previous days, which I now turn and check for mold. After eating the food I prepared last night, I walk outside to give my thanks to nature.

The sun is setting. The short embrace of spring has taken hold of the valley; even the cycle of the moon seems truncated in springtime. I listen to the river crack as it slowly thaws; sometimes large chunks of ice rub together and there is a strained baying. In a week or two I know the ice will be melted away. A barn owl takes flight from a tree, and leaves the branches quivering.

As I turn back to the house, I'm stopped by a tall shadow up near the shed. It is too tall for it to be an animal. Quietly I step into the grove of chestnut trees to observe unnoticed. The silhouette also moves slowly, as if mocking my steps. I can see something long and thin: part of the shadow looks like a rifle. The groaning of the river flips my stomach, a creek of sweat slithers down my back. Everything is silent. The river, too, seems to be holding its breath.

But the shadow continues up the mountain path and then disappears. The sweat has begun to make me feel chilled. I know I must go back into the house before it becomes worse. I take a few steps, then my feet become entangled in undergrowth and I fall, face first, onto the ground. As I push myself up, my fingers press against something hard. In the half-moon light, I can see that it is a skull, not an animal's but a human's. I rush to the house.

As I close the door, I notice the yellow eyes of the owl. They look different than they did only minutes ago.

In late spring, once the weather has warmed and the roads can be traveled upon, I go to Yanji where I buy provisions and share a bed with a woman. Once every month, until winter again dominates the valley, I return to the provincial capital, more to sate my desire of the flesh than to restock my shelves. It has been this way for the past thirty years. Even as a child, long before my father left me at the hotel the autumn I turned eighteen, I would accompany him several times a year to Yanji, which rests seven hundred feet above the valley, twenty-one miles from our farm.

Arriving in the city, my father would press a coin into my palm, then disappear into the hotel. I would go to a grocer in the market and buy seven orange moon cakes. I would set aside the last cake for my father and eat six of them while sitting on the steps of the store, watching the activity in the market. All around, I would see signs in Chinese and Korean.

My father had explained that for many years Koreans had been living here. Like him, they had been brought here by the Japanese army, and then after the war they chose to settle. He had told me that nearly half of the two million people in the region were of Korean heritage, and insisted that I learn his language so I would be able to trade with all the vendors.

Taking my time eating the cakes, I would eye the girl selling brooms and brushes and sponges under the umbrella of a colorful vending cart. When the steps became uncomfortable, I still would not move, but would continue to try and imagine what I might say to her if I could find my courage to cross the street.

Over the years, I would keep my place on the steps and marvel at the changes in the girl's figure, in her face, in her voice as she called out selling her wares. But I never approached her—the correct words, or any words at all, remained wedged in my throat, nearly choking me.

There are times when I walk the entire eight-hour distance to Yanji, leaving long before sunrise and arriving around noon. Today, however, I don't feel up to it. Instead I go to the crossroads, five miles downriver, and look for a ride with one of the truckers who have gathered there. Most of the time, the driver is the same one I have known for many years. I spot his truck on the side of the dirt road. I am fortunate today, for the cabin of the truck is empty and I can sit up front with the driver and not have to squeeze into the truck's bed along with everything he happens to be hauling: from coal to chickens, ears of corn to pig heads.

"Congratulations on surviving another winter," he says, holding out a pack of cigarettes, although he knows I don't smoke.

"You too."

He shifts the truck into gear, hangs his left arm out the window, and we bounce down the rutted road.

"It looks nearly empty." The driver points to the limp burlap bag at my feet.

"It's not as easy as it used to be to find ginseng. I still blame the government for killing off the sparrows. It's a curse."

"You should change trades."

"If it came down to starving, I would still hunt."

"There are many things to hunt."

"There's nothing more rewarding than finding the perfect root."

"Perhaps that's true, but those rewards don't feed you in the winter."

The driver dodges holes, plunges into others, his cigarette bobbling as ashes fall off his work jacket and tumble onto the floor of the truck.

"I'll let you in on a little secret. For the past couple of months I've tripled my income."

"How'd you do that?"

"Hauling people."

"Does that mean I have to start paying you for your service?"

"Hell, no. Besides, these people don't pay me. The government does."

"What are you talking about?"

"Those people crossing the river."

"Who?"

"Look, I'm not some bastard or anything, but those Koreans come here and steal. They've become a nuisance."

"Maybe one of them was in my garden last week?"

"Well, there you are. All you need to do is hand them over to the local authorities and you'll receive your money. Two hundred yuan a person. Man, woman, or child. They don't know who to trust, just give them a little food and they'll follow you anywhere you lead them. Like stray cats."

Neither of us speaks for a while. The dirt road ends and the final ten miles to Yanji are paved.

"I'll tell you what, if you bring people to my truck, I'll haul them for you. Just give me a thirty-percent cut. It's easy money, and by the looks of that bag of yours, you're going to need it."

"I'll think about it."

The driver drops me at a traffic light, but before I jump down from the truck, I hand him a roll of tobacco leaves.

"Thanks for the ride."

"See you next month."

He pulls away, leaving me at my familiar section of the city. Although I have been coming here most of my life, I know very little of this city other than this street and a few others—everything within a couple hundred yards of here: the market where I buy my provisions and sell my ginseng, a few restaurants, a tea house, and this place at whose front door I am now standing, this place that once held such mystery.

I am eighteen. It is the time of year when the rooftops of Yanji are reddened by the chili peppers drying in the early

September sun. My father and I buy the provisions together on this day, and when we have finished, instead of pressing a coin into my hand, my father leads me to the hotel.

After all these years, today my father's the one who stays on the outside; he says that he will wait for me in the tea house across the street.

An unknown smell hits me as soon as I enter the lobby—a whiff of flowers but more pungent, secretive. I stand alone in this strange lobby. Should I sit on one of the red chairs or run out of the hotel? Everything in here looks so clean, none of it seems real. I feel that if I were to touch a chair or a vase or table, it would crumble like a lump of dry soil.

Footsteps creak on the wooden floor. An older woman appears; her eyes and cheeks and lips have been tinted; her nails, too, are red. She seems as mysterious as the scent of this place.

"Your room is two-sixteen, just up the stairs and to the left."

I don't dare question this woman, whose tulip-tipped hand touches me on the shoulder. When I am at the top of the stairs, I pull at my jacket to see if she's left any of her red paint. There is nothing there. The numbers on the doors descend: 219, 217, 215. I stop and think back to what she told me. "Two-sixteen," she said. The number in front of me matches her words, but I'm not sure what to do.

I study the brown wooden door and raise my hand to knock when the door opens. Again I am touched by painted fingers. This woman is different. She takes my winter-like hand and leads me into the room. The room feels stuffy; it is narrow and huge, all at the same time. My cold hand warms in her soft one. She smells of pink and lavender.

"Put your hands on top of mine."

I do as she says. She brings my hands to her face. I pull them away.

"Keep your hands on mine and follow them wherever they go. Don't think, just feel what I feel."

Our hands move to her painted face, to her forehead, then down around the lobes of her perfect ears and along the nape of her long neck. They no longer feel as four. They push away enough of her silk robe to reveal her collarbone, and her throat; they move to her pale shoulders and the robe slips down her arms.

A fiery knot lights below my waist and I'm confused what I'm supposed to do. She holds me and keeps my knees from buckling. I want her to remove my shirt so that I can feel her chest against mine. After I calm down, she takes me across and down her provinces; once more, on the way back up, I feel the tightening below my waist. This time it doesn't catch me off-guard. She smiles and holds me until I recover. Like a large white cloud crawling up the sultry mountains, her robe edges its way back up and she stands before me just as she was when she opened the door. But I will never be the same.

SUMMER

ALL ALONG the three hundred miles of the Tumen, they have returned in flight. Great egrets. Herons. Wood sandpipers. White wagtails. Sparrow hawks. Ringed plovers. Rufous-tailed robins. Others have staggered out from a winter of hibernation. Hedgehogs. Forested bats. Badgers. Raccoon dogs. Asiatic black bears. So, too, has the river been released from its frozen hibernation. The wildlife never comes too close to the thawing water's edge in the higher reaches of the mountains because of the force of the current. Farther downriver, however, where the Tumen begins to settle, a black bear or deer or boar may dab a paw or dip a mouth or wet a nose, cautiously aware of the large chunks of ice flowing past, a single one of which can crush anything in its path.

Down here there are long stretches where the river runs straight and wide and the ice moves more smoothly. But where the river narrows and the bends sharpen—some nearly at right angles—the ice has nowhere to go and becomes jammed until the temperatures rise and melt the pieces into smaller chunks. Then once again they can flow unimpeded, wending their way to the sea.

IN THE COUNTRY across the river, a woman hugs her daughter and whispers this story to her.

Far away and over many mountains, there is a city called Utopia where only tomatoes live. These tomatoes enjoy the best that the country has to offer: the best fertilizers, the best soil, the best greenhouses. Other fruits or vegetables may not enter Utopia. They are kept out so that they do not tarnish the tomatoes in any way.

Outside Utopia, across the first ridges of mountains, live the apples, good apples with bright red skin but white insides. These apples dream of one day becoming completely red; then they too, like the tomatoes, could live in Utopia or at least visit and see all the magnificent monuments built to honor the reddest, ripest, purest tomato of all.

There is a third group in this country of fruit: grapes. The grapes can never ever dream of Utopia; they have no red at all, they have no chance of ever changing color. When they are in the sun they do not ripen, but shrivel and become wrinkled. These grapes are pushed farther and farther away, over the infinite peaks of mountains, mountains which block Utopia's glow and seal the grapes' fate.

Your father, and his father before him, were born grapes—so too were you and I. Soon we must begin to make our way over the mountains and head farther away from Utopia.

Later the young mother must make the journey alone.

A woman and her husband find her on the banks of the river and bring her to their house; they take care of her, hiding her in an old chicken coop. They tell her how they have helped others who escaped from her country, and how they place themselves in great danger by doing so. She believes what they say; they are kind people.

One day, the woman talks to her through the wire cage of the coop.

"What do you plan to do?" the woman asks her.

"I have no plans."

"We can help you find a husband. There are many men in this area looking for a wife."

She doesn't know how to respond; she didn't come here for a husband.

"That would be best for you," the woman advises. "We have helped many women."

The woman's tone is less friendly now; the chicken coop feels less secure. She takes a deep breath, closes her eyes, and when she opens them the woman has walked away.

Two days later she is hidden under stacks of blankets and sacks of corn in the back of a truck. The roads are smooth and in a short time the truck stops. Footsteps, horns blowing, and vendors shouting tell her that she is in a large town. There is a long wait, she may have fallen asleep. Then the truck jerks forward. The husband speaks to her through the cab's rear window.

"I'm going to leave you here with a woman. Her name is Miss Wong. When I stop the truck and knock on the side, you must leave the truck immediately and quickly go inside the building."

It is just like being swept away by the river; she has no control over what is happening. She hears the knock, and as the man has ordered her to do, she hurries into the building. She never sees the woman or the man again and for the next month she never leaves the hotel; her only contact with the outside world is with the men who visit her room.

MISS WONG knows my taste. She knows that I like some tea, iced in summer, lukewarm in autumn; knows that I like to have the woman waiting for me up in the room and that I enjoy the anticipation, the surprise when I open the door. There have been times when the same woman was up there, but that has never happened in consecutive months—never more than twice in a year, unless I request it. I have asked only once. Miss Wong was her name, the same as the proprietress. In order to discourage intimacy, all the women are given her name. So, as I climb the stairs, the one thing I can be certain of is that the woman waiting for me today is called Miss Wong.

I open the door and she is standing with her back to me, in the far left corner by the lamp. She turns around, and although the light is low, I know instantly that I have never seen her before. I can also tell from her rigid stance and the way she looks me in the eye so briefly, that she hasn't been doing this for long. I am unnerved, and start to turn my head away at about the same time she nods toward the door, which I close. There are no locks on the doors—I heard that the proprietress eliminated them after a woman was strangled by a patron. There is not much in the room: the bare walls adorned by scabs of paint, the dim light choked in a storm of dust whenever the lamp is switched on or off. There are no windows. She stands there, her eyes boring into the dingy carpet.

I am the first to move. We are close enough that if I were to reach out my arm, and she hers, our hands would touch. Instead my arms stay at my sides. I can tell that she is young. That is not a problem for me; I prefer young women to those who are closer to my age. Their youth allows me to escape my feelings of growing old.

As I look down past her slender neck, I see childlike breasts through the thin robe. Fifteen. Twenty-five. Fifteen frightens and rejuvenates me; however, I feel safer with twenty-five. I want to ask her age but am not sure I want to know.

She places her hand on my arm; only the palm touches me. I notice how she keeps her fingertips from making contact. Her other hand reaches to the front of my trousers and I push it away, disliking to be rushed. Perhaps it is the hollowness of her eyes, the mistrust in them, that betrays her and makes me realize that she is not from here. Without thinking, I speak to her in Korean.

"I just want to lie with you."

The words sound awkward.

She leads me to the bed and we sit on it; her palm seems cemented to my arm. I expect to see an imprint when she lifts her hand and places it in my own, but there is no imprint, only a cool dampness. Her hand is large, but bony. The tips of her fingers are blackened as if from frostbite, and every time I brush them, she winces.

"I have not seen you here."

"I arrived only last month."

She does not question why I know her language. Perhaps I am not her first client to speak it. Her voice is a low-pitched sparrow's—before it has eaten the berries of the ginseng plant.

I want to turn off the lamp, but for some reason letting go of her hand seems unimaginable. And it is like this, my hand in hers, that I fall asleep; and she, with her eyes open, still has hold of my hand when I awaken hours later.

As I have done on many occasions with others in this same room, I seek her body during the night. She is naked; she must have undressed after I fell asleep. She lies motionless at first, only I am moving. But soon she joins me. When I look down at her, she is not staring over my shoulder at the ceiling or the wall, as many tend to do, but looking directly at me. I stop. Her eyes appear older, as if she has aged in the few hours that I have known her. Beads of sweat loll on her breasts. Collapsing onto her body, I hold her tight in order not to have to meet her eyes. Her ribs form a birdcage against my chest, so fragile; I fear my weight may crush it.

"Do you hurt?"

"No, it was fine."

I did not mean from the sex but from my lying on top of her. I don't correct myself.

"Where are you from?"

I rise up on my arms; she pulls me back on top of her. This time, she is the one who doesn't want to meet my eyes. I think of what the truck driver said to me and won-

41

der what she would be worth——a single root of average ginseng?

"You have nothing to fear," I say.

She doesn't answer. I don't speak any further; she covers herself with the sheet. The lamp continues to burn, waiting for someone to turn it off. The feel of the front of her body pressed against my back tells me she is more relaxed now.

Never have I slept so deeply away from the sounds of the crickets and toads and owls, which carry me to my nightly rest. My desire to rush back to the farm and its reassuring solitude is strangely faint. I turn and take her in my arms.

The room has been paid for in advance, as usual. There is no need to go and see the proprietress, but as I am leaving, I make a point of stopping to say goodbye.

"Until next month, Miss Wong."

"Thank you."

I know from her slight smile and bow of the eyelids that she understands my wish is for yesterday's Miss Wong to be next month's Miss Wong.

WHEN THE Great Leader dies, a sky of cranes swoop from the heavens to carry His body back with them. As they near the land, the thousands of cranes see all of the people wailing and crying lakes upon lakes of tears. The cranes also begin to cry and a fine rain falls on the mourning nation. The cranes pound the air with their wings, and strong winds blow all over the country. Witnessing this deepest of love for the Great Leader, the cranes cannot bring themselves to take Him away. They pick Him up, ever so gently, and fly Him to a heavenly palace built here on Earth, in order that He will always be near His people and forever be their Eternal Leader.

After the death of the Great Leader, a new leader, His Son, inherits the Kingdom of Tomatoes, and he is known as the Dear Leader.

Years before the death of His Father, the mythology of the Dear Leader's life had already begun in a humble log cabin on top of the most sacred mountain, Paekdu.

Halfway up the cabin's window snow has gathered, while overhead a brown swallow soars and dives and sings: "A son has come, a son has come, the son of the Great Leader has come." A double rainbow arches over the cabin, and the swallow, as it flies through the rainbow, is painted a multitude of colors. Red, green, violet, yellow, orange, blue. More brilliant than any bird has ever been. Each time it passes through the rainbow, it is painted again and again. And the swallow soars and dives and sings: "A son has come, a son has come, the son of the Great Leader has come." All through the day, and into the night, the swallow sings, its path lit by a bright star, which shows itself glowing for the first time over the humble log cabin atop Mount Paekdu.

She used to believe these stories, used to carry them around with her as she would a favorite doll. The tale of the birth of the Great Leader's son was her favorite. In her late teens, she would still happily recite this story, which all the children must learn at a very young age. No matter her mood, thinking about the Dear Leader always made her feel good.

Then life in her country began to change—food rations were cut and her husband was no longer paid for his work in the mines. The stories no longer rang true. After her husband was sent to reeducation camp for leading a protest against the government, she would teach the tales to her daughter so she would be prepared when she started school. Her husband never returned home, but she went on praising the Great Leader and Dear Leader; she concealed her emotions and never showed her daughter how she felt. An ability that would later prove vital.

THE WAY the forest watches me is the same way I watch it. All these years, the familiarity usually soothes me. Today, however, it is unsettling. I can feel that I am being watched by more than the trees. I spin around, attempting to catch whoever is there, but I cannot see anyone. I go up the path, down a different one—sitting, standing, pacing. I think of going home, ending the day right here, but I know that I must confront whoever is following me. The smell of a hastily put out campfire leads me up a rocky path to a patch of trampled leaves and ferns. A shack—held together by broken branches, strips of plastic and thin metal—stands waiting for a sneeze to send it tumbling. I don't move any closer; I check in all directions, but still I see no one. I take the bundle of food from my backpack and approach the shack. On the ground, I lay down my offering in hopes it will keep the person away from my house and fields.

Coming down the mountain, hungry and disappointed for having wasted the day, I turn sharply into the path of a farmer. Between shallow breaths, he tells me that he has been looking for his missing bull.

"I'll let you know if I see it."

"I'd appreciate that. There are a lot of strange goings-on around here. I've been farming for decades and the only bull I've lost was years ago to a black bear. This bull disappeared; there's not a trace."

"What else has been happening?"

"Gardens are being raided. Not by animals, but by people. They're picking the food weeks before it is ripe. Whoever's eating it is going to be very sick."

Once again, I wish I were alone.

"If you see anything, I live seven houses west of the second big bend in the river."

"Okay."

"You should carry a gun."

"I have nothing worth taking."

"Your life. You have your life."

"I'll let you know if I find your bull."

I wait while the farmer's head disappears over the rise, and stand there until the day's tranquillity returns.

Usually a woman lingers in my thoughts and on my skin for a day or two after I return home and then she fades, forgotten until the following month. But it's been more than a week since I left her and still she slides in and out of my hunting day and clings to me at night, leaving me unrefreshed in the mornings and with the urge to find an excuse to go back to Yanji immediately. I laugh at myself, fretting to come up with an excuse.

Standing now on one of the many paths made by the feet of my family for more than six decades, I see only trees and shrubs for miles in every direction. Rarely do I catch a glimpse of anyone on my side of the river. Although I have heard that our soldiers patrol the frontier, they stay mostly invisible—unlike the North Koreans. I look across the Tumen.

As a young man, while fishing for chum salmon, I would call over to the North Korean soldiers. Sometimes we would exchange our salmon for fermented cabbage. After the fall of the Soviet Union, Russia and we grew more distant from North Korea, and I heard we stopped our aid. The river became a true barrier—not to be crossed unofficially.

Today, however, North Korea seems to be closer than ever. I can easily see there are many more of her soldiers than usual. Some of them have removed their jackets and are whittling branches into stakes, while others cluster beside the river. I watch them pounding the stakes into the ground every fifteen yards. They wrap a coil around a stake and pull the wire to the next one and wrap it, too, with the coil. They appear to be shoring up the border.

As I follow the stakes and coils along the river's opposite side, I am hoping to feel one of the rare breezes coming off the Tumen's waters, which remain cool, never completely warming up, even in the summer's heat. Just before the river curves northward, I stop. It is not the North Korean soldiers that steal my attention, but a mountain across the way. Mount Kosong is stripped and exposed, all forty-five hundred feet of it, as if in a single night a million people descended on it—and each one of them uprooted a tree and hauled it away. Tomorrow I will go to Yanji and ask her how this could have happened. The first trace of sunlight is now on the eastern side of Mount Kosong; I wonder if that side, too, lies bare.

.   .   .

"Firewood," is all she says.

"It is as if all the trees have suddenly been cut."

"You haven't been paying attention."

"I observe the mountains and the trees all the time."

"But you're looking at them up close. Step back and look."

I say nothing. Like the last time, she moves away to her side of the bed when we talk about her country; her back shields her face from mine. I stare at the hills of her spine and I think about hiking them with my fingers.

"Soup," she says.

"Are you hungry?"

"The bark of the trees is used for making soup."

I let the meaning of her words sink in.

"If you peel away the bark and boil it you can make a bitter, light brown broth."

I wonder what kind of bark they boil: the tight grayish bark of an ash or the barks of pine and cedar, which are reddish-brown inside and leave a powdery dust you can brush or blow away.

"But now you have food."

"Yes, but when I first came here, I used to break apart my food into small pieces before I could eat it. Cookies, bread, crackers. All of it."

I try to follow what she is saying.

"I would be so hungry but still I would take the time, the last of my energy, to pick through the food. The fear I had for what was inside was greater than the fear of starvation. It took more than a month before I stopped analyzing each bite. Even today, when I taste something crunchy, I hesitate:

I think maybe there's a piece of glass or a fish hook or one of many other things you put in the food that you give to us."

I don't like how I am feeling. The ripples of her spine remain before me, her words bounce off the wall she's facing and careen back across her body. It is late in the night, a time when I often have the urge to grab my clothes and sneak out of the room, the pull of my farm and the mountains much too strong to resist. Yet next to me is this woman whose name I don't know, whose worries are so foreign to me.

"Why do you think we would do that to your food?"

"That is what we are taught. On propaganda posters, in schools, and every morning over the loudspeakers we would hear the praises of the government and warnings that you will poison us with your food, that your shoes will rot our feet, your hats will make our hair fall out."

"That's ridiculous."

"Not if it's the only thing you ever hear. There are many things you couldn't understand. We wander around here scared, but we have to trust you. What else can we do? Stay in North Korea and die of hunger or die in a reeducation camp?"

"Do you trust me?"

"Do I have a choice?"

ALL HER life the government has provided her with everything through a public distribution system: clothes, grain, apples. Private shops or markets are unknown to her. The stature of a person is measured by the purity of his rice ration—the lower one's stature, the more barley or maize is mixed in with their rice. Only those in Utopia receive the wholeness of rice. Even last year, before her husband lost his job in the mines and was imprisoned, her family never received more than half of their grain in rice.

Now the government has implemented a two-meal-a-day policy, and in 1995 that is cut to six ounces of rations a day and cut further still to two ounces per person each day. The whole world is mired in famine, the government tells the citizens over the loudspeakers daily. Millions and millions of people in South Korea and China are unemployed and their lives are in much worse condition than ours. She knows nothing of other people in other countries, only knows that she and her daughter, this whole village, are without food, and that winter is coming soon.

With a large stone she crushes the corncobs, pounding and mashing them into a powder. From the powder she makes a heavy gruel, and this is what she and her daughter eat until the corncobs run low, not only in her house, but in the entire village. The government, however, issues an order proclaiming it a crime to eat only corncob powder—half of the gruel must be made up of rice root.

Weeks into the ban, the police take away a man down the alleyway from her house, for daring not to mix his corncobs. Several days pass before she sees a poster commanding the people to be at the village's entrance at ten in the morning on the upcoming Saturday.

She knows what that means and briefly she thinks of leaving behind her daughter, hiding her in the house. But she fears what would happen if she is caught.

They go to the entrance on that Saturday, a warm, sunny day. She can see her neighbor tied to a post by the wall, his hands roped behind his back. Standing in the middle of the villagers, she has a clear view of him from his chest up. She hopes the people in front will shield her small daughter.

A pronouncement is read by the village head. As he reads, she squeezes her daughter tight. She is tense with anticipation and looks at the few clouds in the sky. Nothing happens. Her daughter is trying to wriggle free. Suddenly a man pushes his way through the crowd toward her, creating space so all can see. He reaches out and grabs her daughter and drags her to the front of the crowd. In seconds, a single shot rings out.

SHE NEEDS help in navigating the city and has asked me to walk with her. She has been outside of the hotel alone only once since she has come to Yanji. I tell her my knowledge of the city is limited, but she points out that even my limited knowledge is greater than hers.

I arrange to meet her at the east end of the market in an hour. The market is the only place that comes to mind. I have been dealing with the same ginseng vendors there for years, the same buyers with whom my father dealt.

Now I must cross the wide streets lane by lane. The traffic, the shrieking horns, puts me on edge. Already I am exhausted. The signs in both languages and the people slipping in and out of two tongues, like one does with pairs of trousers, seem to close in on me. Why did I agree to meet her?

I buy some goods that I need to take back with me, which carves away only a few minutes. She said one hour. I try to calculate the amount of time that has passed, but I am at a loss without the signs of nature to guide me.

My arms are full of packages when I see her. Draped in sunlight and clothed, she is a different person—no longer fifteen; it seems impossible to have imagined it. My self-consciousness has lifted. Her face carries the strain of a difficult life.

"Are you hungry?"

"No, let's walk," she says.

I leave my packages with one of the vendors and we move through the market with all its colors and bumping bodies. It's too noisy to speak. About halfway through, we hear a loud commotion. I try to catch a glimpse of what is happening.

"Let's go."

She walks away; her mood is like the weather in the Changbai Mountains, different from one minute to the next. I make it out of the market and catch up to her; I am sweating, my shirt is branded to me. I stop her.

"Why did you run off like that?"

"I don't like crowds and people pushing. I had to get out of there."

We stand on the street, the heat in the city clawing at me.

"Have you ever been to Victory Park?" I ask her, re-membering vaguely the park that my father once took me to. "The park has some trees, a little shade."

We walk toward the large traffic circle up the street. Five or six lanes embrace a small park that sits on an incline in the middle.

"Are we going there?" she asks.

"No, Victory Park is much larger."

"You don't like cars, do you?"

"I'm just not used to them."

With her arm wrapped around mine, she pulls me into the dizzying stream of cars and trucks and vans and donkey-carts and buses. Only when we have reached the center does she release my arm and it occurs to me: am I not the one who is supposed to be taking care of her?

We step into the park and see a small pagoda with some benches scattered around it; we are the only people here. I can see Victory Park across the way.

"That's the park where we are going." I point to the other side of the circle. I realize that I don't want to go. "Why don't we stay right here? It seems pleasant."

"But we will have to cross the traffic again to return."

Something of a smile sneaks to her lips, which I haven't seen before, and for the moment I savor it.

"Let's sit down."

I lead her to one of the benches; the cement is cool, like a rock up in the mountains. The traffic is less noisy here and I am able to speak in a normal tone of voice.

"Why did you come here to Yanji?"

"I heard that it was best to stay away from the Chinese villages along the river. In a city it is a little easier to blend in."

"How did you know about Miss Wong's place?"

"A man took me to her. If we make it into your country, there are people in the cities looking for us. Some of them want to help, others want to harm us. All have something to gain from us—like Miss Wong."

Like me, I think, unable to look her way.

"I'm better off than many. Most of them sleep in abandoned buildings or in the mountains. I have food and a place to sleep."

"But you're always scared."

"Yes, I will always be on the run. The only place where I could be safe is in South Korea, but almost no one ever succeeds in getting there. If we are caught, we are sent back. In North Korea I was also on the run, living in fear. I had no choice in that. At least this is a fear I have chosen."

Pigeons poke around our feet searching for something to eat and, frustrated, they move to the steps of the pagoda.

"But they will never take me back."

The conviction of what she is saying wrenches my eyes from the pigeons. She sits there, but has disappeared inside her words. There is so much distance between us.

"If they do catch me, I will take this."

She reaches inside her blouse and pulls out a small plastic pouch hanging from her neck by a shoestring.

"Before they hand me over, I will be dead."

"What is it?"

"Rat poison. Almost everyone carries something. Glass or safety pins to swallow. Cyanide, if they can find it. They are the lucky ones, the ones with the cyanide. It is a horrible way to die, but it's much quicker."

The cement bench has become uncomfortable and I want to stretch my back. I don't.

"The journey to South Korea is long and dangerous and can take months or years. Maybe I will try it, but first I will try to survive here."

I think how each year of hunting allows me to endure the winter. My entire life is centered around the seasons. When spring arrives I immediately begin preparing for the following winter. The continued existence I know is nothing like the existence she speaks of.

She stands and walks over to the pigeons. The birds cautiously gather around her. Then she begins to stomp her feet, stomp, stomp, until every last pigeon has taken to the air, leaving her there on the pagoda steps all alone. I sit awhile longer before I decide to speak.

"Let's eat something, my ride is leaving soon."

"Why don't you stay tonight?"

"I have to go back to work."

"What is it you do?"

Never in all my years of going to Miss Wong's have I been asked a question so personal. I change the subject.

"What do you want to eat?"

"Some hot pot."

"That's fine."

She takes the lead, and we cross the traffic circle and within minutes we are back near the market. I notice that she has turned around to look at a young boy, perhaps the dirtiest boy I have ever seen, huddled between a video arcade and a shoe repair shop.

"Do you know him?"

She looks again at the young boy. He is without shoes, the toes on his left foot are missing.

"No."

She glances at him one last time.

When the two bowls of hot pot arrive we quickly begin to eat the beef, cabbage, and potato stew. Before she has finished, she excuses herself and goes out the door. I watch her through the window. I see her putting some money in the kid's hand. How many hours of my time with her did she give him? A minute later she returns. We say nothing: both of us continue eating. I can't let it alone.

"How old is he?" I ask.

"How old do you think?"

I like that she denies nothing.

"Twelve," I answer.

"Seventeen, maybe older."

I think for a moment that maybe we are talking about two different boys.

"We call them *kotchebi*: flower swallows. Some of them sneak back and forth across the river, take money or food to their families, if their families are still alive. Many of them are alone, so they often come here in small groups and scour the countryside looking to find a menial job, or they come to the city to beg or steal. That was what was going on in the market. Two boys stole food and they were caught. That is why I ran away."

"They cross the river so easily?"

"They cross late at night and hope the soldiers don't spot them. Recently, the soldiers have also become hungry and, at times, can be bribed. A few years ago there was an order from my government to arrest these kids— 'vagabonds,' the government calls them—and they were put in camps."

I lift my cup of tea and realize that I have drunk it all.

"Usually the younger kids are released or sent to a detention camp for a while. Sometimes they are sold here in China. Young people are very valuable as cheap or free labor for farms as well as sex shops. If they are lucky a good person helps them. They get to stay in the person's house, but almost all the time they are locked in a room underground or in a closet."

"Why do you call them flower swallows?"

"Because, like a flower swallow, which jumps from flower

to flower, these kids dart from place to place. They are small and frail; many of them just stop growing."

"Stop growing?"

"If a plant doesn't have water, the same happens," she answers.

"But plants don't stop growing, they die."

"And that is what will happen to that boy outside if he doesn't have some food. Your country is the drop of water that we need to give us a chance to survive."

She eats the last of her hot pot and asks when I must leave.

"Soon."

"When will you come back?"

"Next month."

"Why not sooner? I would like to talk with you."

She startles me again. Why would she want to talk with me? I with the clumsy tongue, who stands here thinking about my farm and the mountains, places far away from her?

"I told you I must work. My home is a day's travel from here."

"Next time we have to walk farther and talk. There are so many things I want you to understand."

HAVE YOU *ever watched a child go off on her first day of school, and then, little by little, she shrivels and dies before your eyes?*

Your child's first day, she is nervous, as are you, standing outside the school gate, but you urge her on and she walks past the gate and under the sign: LET'S BE THE TRUE CHILDREN OF OUR LOVED AND RESPECTED FATHER AND LEADER, KIM JONG IL. *You wait until she enters the school building, then you leave. On your way home, you pass the garbage piles out on the street and you check to see that no one is watching and you find some food and you know you can make a meal for the both of you on this most special of days and you go home and from the scraps you do create something.*

You meet your child back at the same gate where you left her and the two of you walk home and she talks excitedly about her day and you eat together, but all the time you are silent, for you know where the meal came from, know that tomorrow is going to be a repeat of today and the next day a repeat of that.

The following week, your daughter goes on a school trip to the neighboring town square, from where she will return in the afternoon and tell you how she, and many school kids from all over the area, saw a man with a rope around his neck and his feet near but never touching the ground, how he hung there for a very long time, all the time moving side to side, as if the wind was blowing him back and forth, like a puppet. The children return to the school and learn a new song about the Dear Leader, the teacher playing the accordion, and now your child sits in your house and sings it for you:

61

We are happy, we have nothing to envy.
Long live General Kim Jong Il,
the wise leader of our nation.
You are the sun of our solar system
and we orbit around you.

The same lines over and over and you pretend as though you are listening, but you aren't, and you try not to believe what she has told you, wanting to scold her for telling terrible lies, but you don't do that either, because you know that what she says is the truth.

By winter your child stops going to school and each day she joins you looking for food and firewood, each of you going in a different direction, and you meet at home and see what the other has gathered. One day you see your child's teacher, but before you recognize her, you fight with her over the mugwort you have found. When you are certain that it is the teacher, you let go of the mugwort as if it were a hot ember, and then you understand that it is not only your child who is not in school, no one is in school, all of the villagers are out doing the same. Survival has become your livelihoods.

Your child stops growing and you feed her tree-bark soup and sometimes rice root, even though you know that rice root can make her blind, never passing through her, just sitting there, as it does in your stomach, a stone, an unbreakable stone. Season after season this goes on. On the birthdays of the Great and Dear Leaders, and other revered holidays, there are still no rations.

One day you are up in the mountains, alone, and you see two soldiers eating and drinking with two other men, they are eating rice by the handful. You haven't had rice, haven't seen it for so long and you try to remember the texture, but it doesn't come to you.

Without warning, the soldiers stop talking, and the other two men have fallen to the ground and the soldiers walk away, down the mountain. You wait, minutes or hours, only the silence tells you it is okay to breathe again, and you hurry over to the men. They are sprawled there, it could be only a couple of drunks passed out in the middle of eating, could be, as long as you don't look above to where their faces should be. You concentrate so hard that your head thunders and you try to keep your eyes on the rice scattered across the mossy carpet. At first you pick up the rice grain by grain, stuff it into your mouth, but each grain makes you crave another and you begin to grab and eat whatever lies nearby—pebbles, rice, twigs. You scour the ground to make certain that you have left not a grain of rice behind, and then you see their filthy hands, the rice that they hold, like freshly fallen snow into a bucket of coal. Using your fingers, you eat from the bowls of their hands, you can't eat fast enough and then the bowls are clean, only a few scattered grains stick to them. You have had too much, your stomach is not used to all this food, but the stomach and mind are out of sync and the animal in you presses your face down and you eat the last of the rice directly from the hands.

Now it is over, it is done, and you are again a person, a person who begins to cry and gasp, unable to catch a single breath because, for the first time since the soldiers killed the men, you think of the child, your child, waiting at the bottom of the mountain, waiting to see what you have found for this day's meal, and you know there is nothing.

DURING THE June barley rains, the river crawls up the slight slope to the west of my land and comes within yards of my cornfield. Only once has the river come to my door. Today the Tumen, like the sky above, is at its cloudiest; the tips of its rapids reach up to touch the leaves of the oldest willows.

Out of the side of my right eye, I catch a glimpse of an object rushing downstream. Large and distended, like the massive bladder of a prehistoric animal, it churns in the current of the Tumen. Could it be a body? I can't imagine what it would be doing in the river. Certainly the waters are wild enough to drown a person. That has happened many times but always below, where the Tumen flows near villages and towns. I think of the farmer's missing bull. Although the body doesn't look like a bull's, the possibility is easier to accept.

Soon another large object goes by; this time closer. Heading directly for the cluster of trees, the object—like the previous one—is bloated, monster-like, with bulging eyes. Again I tell myself it cannot be human. Days in the water can contort an object into any shape, I reason. As the mind of a hunter can talk himself into believing anything that he wants to believe, so too can the words of a woman.

Long before I come upon it, I smell the carcass of the bull and instantly know that my day is over; I will not be able to regain my hunting rhythm. I take one of the red pieces of cloth and hold it over my nose and mouth. The bull has been left to the insects. It doesn't appear that a large animal—bear or mountain lion—killed it. I notice no sign of the bull being dragged, nor is there any damage to the undergrowth.

Retracing my morning steps, I see a pair of blue-gray dragonflies mating in midair. It will be several weeks before the dragonflies turn red, signalling the beginning of autumn. I am with my thoughts. Two months into the hunting season and there is not much to show for my effort. Back home, a plastic sheet with this month's drying ginseng is less than a fifth covered and none of the roots are more than a dozen years old. The climb down is long, the gnats and flies and fleas vie for my attention; nearer to the river the mosquitoes join in.

I see the farmer out in his field and realize I should let him know about his bull. I open the tamarisk gate and we meet in the lane to his house.

"Where did you find it?" he asks, before I have a chance to speak.

"The third path to the right, off the main one where I ran into you. There's not much left of the bull."

"It was the Koreans."

I don't say anything.

"The feeling in the air has a bad, bad odor to it. I used to have some pity for them."

I think of my lover and whether it's right to feel sorry for her. I think of my father and uncle and wonder where that leaves me. I start to leave.

"Thank you for your troubles."

I nod to him.

"Soon, when the river is lower, more of them will cross," the farmer says, spitting to the side.

The forest is so entwined with my family's history that I have come to view the trees as my siblings.

High up in the Changbai range, during the two and a half centuries of the Qing Dynasty, my father would tell me, the greatest hunters scoured this forest for Emperor's Ginseng: the purest of ginseng. This finest root was only for the emperor, and if it was discovered in the hands of a lesser hunter, he would have been flogged and exiled, even beheaded.

When the Qing Dynasty ended early in the twentieth century, so too did their ban on hunting the root. But in my ancestral homeland there never was a ban, and my family had been hunters for many generations—until the Japanese army occupied Korea and invaded China. At the hands of the Japanese, my grandparents, along with thousands and thousands of their fellow Koreans, were forced across the river into China 'in support of Japan's expansionist dreams. Over the next decade, my grandfather labored in the fields and factories. He knew well the Japanese: as early as 1911, they had stripped Koreans of their names, their language, and their culture.

As the Second World War entered its final year, the Japanese army conscripted many Koreans, including my grandfather. He and my grandmother urged my father and uncle to flee high into the mountains among these ancient trees. While my grandfather went into the army, my grandmother was sent off to Mongolia to work in a factory; I never met either of them.

But according to my father, his hiding brought about two fortuitous discoveries that would change the course of his life. Spread across the forest floor, my father and uncle found ginseng roots as plentiful—and their quality just as good—as the roots back in their homeland. They began spending their days hunting ginseng, reviving our family tradition. And then one day my father saw a young woman washing bamboo shoots in a stream. He went upstream, keeping an eye on her as he drank from the fresh water. Long after his thirst had been quenched, he kept drinking while trying to think of something to say to her. Finally, it was she who spoke first.

"Don't you know that the war is over?"

"Over?"

"It ended more than a month ago. It is safe for you to return to the valley."

"How do you know I am hiding?"

"Because I know you've been up here for a long time."

"I've never seen you."

"That doesn't mean I couldn't see you," the young Chinese woman told him.

AGAIN HER daughter helps her mother hunt for food and firewood. The sun is down and her mother has returned home with only a handful of reeds and some firewood. She puts the reeds in a pot of water to soak and waits, but her daughter doesn't return. She knows that her daughter started walking south this morning, but that was only the starting point; she could have wandered in any direction. She has taught her daughter to walk until noon, then rest a little before turning back.

With only a few hours of firewood, she conserves it and sits in the dark, cold kitchen, hoping that her daughter has found something to eat. The village has sunk into its nightly rhythms: low voices; an occasional popping cinder from a fire; a muffled clang from a pot. The slice of the moon is framed by the window when she finally hears her daughter at the door. She can't see her, but knows immediately that she has been crying.

"What happened?"

Her daughter doesn't speak. She leads the child to the center of the kitchen and pats her face and head, as much out of love as in search of a cut or a lump or dried blood. She finds nothing and, relieved, starts preparing the fire. The wood is thin and damp; it takes a long while for it to catch. As the flames begin to stretch the light, her daughter speaks.

"I was in the tall grass, digging for roots, and I lost my badge of the Great Leader."

"Do you remember where the grass is?"

"It's a long way from here. I got lost. But I remembered what you told me to do. I walked away from the mountain."

"Did you see any soldiers?"

"I saw two, but they didn't stop me."

"Without your badge you cannot go out. I will have to find you another one."

The next morning she leaves her daughter behind. As she passes dead bodies on the streets and on the paths leading up the mountain, she slows her pace. She looks around to see if anyone is watching her. If the body is lying on its back she can easily see if there is a badge. If, however, the body is lying face down she must take the branch that she is carrying and wedge it under the body, lifting it up just enough to see if there is a badge. Until now, there have been none.

This is the tenth body today. As she stuffs the branch under it, the branch is suddenly torn from her hands. The man turns over and jumps up. He is wild-looking with dirt and leaves tangled in his hair—but on his jacket is a badge. He hits her with the branch, she breaks away, but he pursues her, hitting her over and over until finally she is free and leaves him on the path waving the branch and screaming.

Hiding in some thick bushes, she knows that this day-to-day humiliation will be with her forever. She realizes that in this country even the living are dead.

She is so weak from the lack of food that the smallest task is the largest chore. Something as easy as dusting a picture, even the picture of the Great Leader, is like hauling a load of stones up a cliff.

But she has to find something to eat, and she sets out for the mountains, again alone; her child hasn't left the house for weeks. As she is leaving she sees a man looking into her window. She has seen him and other Party members doing this before, at her neighbors', and ignores him. When she returns home she's surprised to find the man inside her house, just sitting against the wall; her daughter is on the floor where she left her, balled up in her nearly constant sleep. The man doesn't move and she thinks he too is sleeping. She goes and hides the oak leaves and acorns. When she turns around the man is standing, not more than a foot away. Does he want her food, her body? He wants neither. He grabs her by the arm, nearly dragging her to the far wall, and shoves her face against the framed picture of the Great Leader and holds her face there. Something warm drips from above her eye, down past her nose. He presses harder and harder and she thinks she will suffocate or her neck will snap. When he releases her, she keeps her head down waiting for his next move, but nothing happens. She hears him speak:

"Never again allow the picture of the Great Leader to be soiled."

The door slams; she leans against the wall and stays there for a very long time. When she finally turns around, she is thankful to see her daughter still asleep on the floor.

There is only one other picture in the house, a frameless photo of her husband and daughter, whose face is half covered by her father's mining helmet. The mining helmet. How distant those days are. Days when they had regular food rations. Then the electricity disappeared in the country and soon afterward he too was gone. A flood was followed by two years with little rain, and many of the country's crops were destroyed.

Now the only reminder she has of her husband is the curled-up picture, hanging on the wall opposite the Great Leader's. Any photo, other than of His son, is forbidden to share a wall with one of the Great Leader. It is on this night, after she has cleaned many times the picture of the Great Leader, that she wakes her daughter and tells her the story about the tomatoes, apples, and grapes. But they have no time to leave and cross the mountains because, early the next morning, the man returns with two others. They examine the picture; it is clean, but they take her outside anyway, leaving her child alone in the house.

Through the village they parade her. Although she sees no one, she knows everyone is watching her and waiting until she is out of sight. In no time, they will be searching her house, searching for food or something that they can burn. No one will take in her daughter; she is just another mouth to feed. She thinks, as she is forced onto a truck, that her daughter will die. This realization bludgeons any fear.

AS I AM ON my way out, Miss Wong, the proprietress, invites me for some tea. She has never done this before in all the years I have been coming here. Tea is served on arrival, never upon leaving.

The tea is iced, as I like it in summer. She sits opposite me, this woman who has always looked about sixty; her fingernails are painted as red as when I first met her back in my late teens.

"So, how is the hunting this year?"

"Very slow. Each year it is more and more difficult to find the best roots."

"It must be lonely out there."

"I love the solitude, that's why I live there."

"Winters are so long, though."

"Yes, they are. That makes the hunting season all the more special."

"I've heard you have been seeing Miss Wong outside of here."

The abruptness of her words startles the truth from me.

"Yes, sometimes for lunch."

"You know that I don't permit my women to see their customers. It confuses matters."

"Yes, I'm aware of that. I'm sorry."

I think about how I am supposed to meet her later this morning.

"You have always been a very good customer and I

greatly appreciate your business, but I can't allow this to continue. However, I will offer you a compromise."

"Which is what, Miss Wong?"

"I will sell her to you. It would be beneficial for us all. For her in particular. As you know, they are repatriating the Koreans who are here illegally and also arresting anyone who houses or helps them."

I glance at Miss Wong, thinking of this unusual relationship we have.

"Are you from across the river, Miss Wong?"

"My parents came from there, brought along by the Japanese army, like your family, I believe."

"Yes."

Neither of us says anything; we drink our jasmine tea. I finish my tea and get up.

"I'll have to think about your offer. I will give you my answer next month."

"I'm sure we can work out a fair price."

How has it come to this, buying and selling people as if they were cattle? These days it seems that bodies in the river and stripped mountains are more abundant than fifty-year-old ginseng roots. But what about her stories? Could she be exaggerating? And Miss Wong has even more to gain. Yet, if I don't buy her, what will that mean?

Despite Miss Wong's admonishment, I wait for her. Across the street, I see an old woman with puppies; I'm sure she's the same one I've seen before, I cross the street and check the two skinny dogs. A sign with 10 *yuan* written on it leans against a box. I remove two five *yuan* bills from my pocket and give them to the woman.

"Which do you want?"

They both look about the same; I choose the dog with more black than white.

"I must go and pick up my supplies. I will be back for the dog shortly."

She closes the lid of the box, clasping the money tightly in her hands; she begins to fold the bills in half, and half again, doing so until they are in compact squares. She pays no attention to me as she lights a candle, tilting it over the small square of bills, not much larger than a coin.

The hot wax drips onto the bills, drop after drop until they have a double coating. While the wax cools, the old woman opens a bottle of water. She then places the waxed bills in her mouth and swallows them with the water. I don't know what to say; I turn my eyes to the dogs, one of which is mine.

We are walking several blocks away from the hotel. I tell her about the old Korean woman.

"She was selling puppies and when she takes the money, she folds, waxes, and then swallows it. Isn't that strange?"

"No. If she is caught crossing back over the river, no matter what the soldiers decide to do with her, she will still have the money she earned. She probably doesn't swallow all the money, so that way she can pay off the soldiers."

"You make it sound so casual."

"Not casual, just people trying to stay alive."

Surviving. How drastically the width of a river can affect its interpretation.

She stops and stares into the window of an electronics store; televisions are playing silent images. This has happened before on our walks; I stand back and let her look for as long as she wants. Somehow I feel as if I am intruding on one of her most private moments. I'm not sure what to do with myself. With so many screens in the window, so many different flickering images, it is impossible to concentrate on one. The televisions perplex me and leave me feeling trapped. More people have started to crowd around the window.

She breaks me out of my trance.

"We must go. There is someone following us," she says.

"Following us?"

"We must go."

She takes off at a fast pace; I try to keep up. I glance back to see who might be there.

"Just keep going. He's across the street."

There are so many people across the street, but I am able to spot him immediately. A large man with a dark jacket and pants, dressed not so differently from the others, but he stands out. He watches us and we walk faster. The man keeps pace. We cross two smaller side streets.

"Should we go into a store?"

"No, they will find me."

"They?"

"There is always more than one."

As if they heard her, a car screeches around the corner

and two men spring out and come rushing toward us. I grab her by the arm and run. I feel as if we will fall head-first, but my agility surprises me. We have reached the market. After about a hundred yards, everything begins to look familiar; I feel as though I am a boy again, and perhaps this is what spurs me up the cement steps and through the yellow door of the small grocery store. Before I know it we are standing in front of a shelf of moon cakes. The cakes have been occupying the same spot for decades, it seems, although the shelf is lower now.

"We will be safe here." I am breathing heavily.

She doesn't speak; she too is out of breath. I notice the small lump under her shirt and am reminded of the poison. I wonder, if we had been caught, whether she would have taken it as she declared she would. I can't imagine what might have happened to me.

We go into the back of the shop and hide near the tins of tea. From here I see the shop's owner sitting behind the counter. He is the same man who would sometimes give me an extra cake, but always a flavor other than orange. I turn to her.

"Who are they?"

"Agents."

"North Korean? What are they doing over here?"

"They are looking for us who have escaped. When they catch us, they take us to the border crossing. Every week, in the city of Tumen, there are trucks filled with North Koreans who are handed over at the border."

"Miss Wong said that they are repatriating them."

"Some of the people are instantly killed in the town

square, others are sent to camps, and the luckiest go back and scour the mountains for something to eat."

The shop owner remains behind the counter. Several minutes pass before I edge my way to the front of the shop.

"It will be okay. They must be gone," I tell her after looking out the front window.

I go over and pick out a half-dozen moon cakes. The owner gently places them into a paper bag, as if they were treasured items. Even as a boy I enjoyed the care that he took with the cakes. When he hands me the bag, the owner says:

"Still buying orange."

"Yes, after all these years."

I lead her down the steps. Although we are only a few minutes' walk to the hotel, I find her a taxi and hand her the paper bag of cakes.

Hurriedly, I gather my supplies and start on my way home, needing to escape this city. With my arms and knapsack bulging, I keep to the side streets in fear that the agents are nearby. I don't go back for the puppy. The day has already been too long. In the coming winter months, on occasion I will think about not picking up the puppy, but I will never dwell on it.

IT WASN'T always this way.

The summer of the frog, her husband still works in the coal mines and often receives extra rations from the government in exchange for providing a vital resource for the country.

August has been more like June, cooler than normal. Her husband returns home from his week in the mines, late on Saturday night. Their daughter is four, and is well into her night's sleep when her husband walks through the door. A dinner of cold porridge and dried fish are on the table but he ignores it, which is unusual for him. He is always hungry after the twelve-mile walk home for his one day off each week, and exhausted from his days in the mine and from his nights, which must be devoted to memorizing speeches of the Great and Dear Leaders.

He clutches his helmet against his chest; his hands cover it like a lid on a pot. He smiles at her, a tired but warm smile, and goes into the sleeping room, kneels by the side of the mat where their daughter lies.

"You shouldn't wake her," she says after him, not meaning it, for she knows it would make both of them happy if he did.

"I have something for her."

"In the helmet?"

"Yes."

He talks to their daughter until she wakes up. He tells her that he has a surprise for her.

"Where? What is it?"

"It's in the helmet."

"What is it?"

He turns the helmet around, all the time covering it with his hands, and sets it on the floor. There is a slight bumping noise inside the helmet; she is as curious as their daughter is to know what is inside. When he lifts the helmet, a frog jumps out; frantically it hops around the floor, the three of them following it, close enough to see the panic pounding in its throat. Her husband corners and scoops up the frog.

"Give me your hands."

The child obeys.

"I'm going to open my hands slowly, just enough for you to touch the frog."

Their daughter puts a finger in between his palms and works in the rest one at a time, but she is uncertain whether or not she feels it.

"Did you touch it?"

"I think so."

"Hold your hands like this, and when the frog is in there, close your hands."

She hesitates.

"Watch your mother," he says, placing the frog in her cupped hands.

Although she doesn't care for frogs, she masks her aversion. She expects something wet and slimy, like cold, boiled cabbage, but it doesn't feel like that; the skin is rough and, down along its hind legs, bumpy. The frog bounces, tickles her palms, and she feels its pulse. *Pit. Pit. Pit.* Quick beats against her own thrumming pulse.

She tells their daughter to hold out her palms as she has done, and she transfers the frog into the little girl's small hands. Her daughter smiles and says that she wants to see the frog, and her father tells her that in the morning they will make a house for it.

While he eats his dinner, she falls asleep next to their daughter. The frog is under the overturned mining helmet, the heartbeat is still in her hands.

YEARS AGO I watched, through these same binoculars, the trains passing on their side of the river, the way the smoke jumped into the air, taking longer to dissipate in winter than in summer. What used to be two or three times a day has dwindled to one or two times a month. There is no more engine leading the way, only a single car, a flatbed with an engine in the middle, people crammed onto it with their legs dangling over the sides. I follow the train as it disappears in and out of patches of trees; I can make out figures and colors, but not faces. The train moves slowly; I keep the binoculars on it for several minutes.

Once the train has entered a tunnel, I lower the binoculars and focus them anew on the fields of corn and the riverbank opposite me. Several scrawny goats come into view, poking through the brown weeds along the river. Near them, two soldiers are on their knees digging in what appears to be a garden. Smoke from a small fire catches my eye and I stop, readjust the binoculars, and see another soldier and a young girl. I steady my elbows on a rock and observe the two of them. The soldier appears to be screaming at the girl. His hand is raised as if he is about to strike her, but he doesn't. The girl is small—the soldier himself doesn't look very large, certainly not the imposing figure that I have imagined. His hand touches the girl's chest and stays there. I have no idea how long it remains; I put down my binoculars and hurry back to my house.

Now she has a price on her, a value, something I can buy, not just rent for a night or two and then leave behind and visit again whenever I have the urge. This changes everything. And the price for her, ounce for ounce, is so much less than what I hunt and sell.

Is it by weight that the proprietress sells her? If not, how does she determine the price? And what if I do take her up on her offer, what could possibly come of it, other than trouble? Years ago I shared my house with a woman; not even a month went by before I knew I was trapped, knew that I had made a terrible mistake. If the snows of winter had not chained the both of us to the farm, I would have made her leave.

The more I think about it, the more certain I am that the proprietress and she have planned this. The thought nags at me, not only because I suspect I am being deceived, but also because it's disrupting my work here in the mountains, which will soon come to an end for another year. These valuable moments are being wasted thinking about a woman——a woman without a name, a woman with all those endless stories, a woman who has become my lover.

Down from the mountain, I stand beside the river and wonder if the soldiers I saw last month have finished wiring the entire length of the Tumen. No longer do I see them in such great numbers; they must have gone back inside their foxholes. I watch the river flow. The nights are becoming cooler, typical for late August. A couple more weeks left for the crickets to sing; after that, not much remains of the hunting season. It will be time to bring in the corn, chili peppers, squash, and pumpkins, and then all the brilliant colors of autumn will give way to the anemic shades of winter.

I try to blot out the ongoing debate in my head.

FROM THE shoulders of the mountains, all the way past the hunter's farm, the Tumen doesn't rest. It cleanses itself, so clean that a swath of silver from a passing school of fish flashes like a sword catching a slice of the sun.

The river downstream loses its energy and the current slows, nearly stopping in places as the Tumen crawls between the towns and villages that dot its banks. Its angle of descent is not steep enough to give it the speed necessary to fend off waste. The industrial cities, on both sides of the river, are too much for the Tumen; by the time the river reaches the city that shares its name, a person standing on its banks must squint to see any sign of the bottom.

Within the past week, as summer races into autumn, the river has receded more than a foot from its banks, and the larger rocks, shined smooth from their centuries of burnishing, are beginning to poke out of the water. Soon the vipers will lie on these rocks for a final time before heading into the mountains to hibernate.

I SET OUT on this fine autumn morning, the time of year when I leave and return home without the sun, when only at midday am I able to dream that summer is still in the valley. However, to imagine this, I must ignore the many truths that lie in front of me.

Although the sun has been out for more than an hour, it is still too low to provide much light in the forest. I move noiselessly, so as not to disturb anything.

The closer to the end of the hunting season, the stronger I am, and after more than two hours up among the redwoods I find my breathing is hardly out of stride. The gnats have disappeared, the cold shoving them down into the valley where they will live out their final days. I pick, and eat, some of the edible plants: gooseberries, wild garlic, hollyhock.

Even in these last weeks of an unsuccessful hunting season, I remain optimistic. In my backpack I carry a wool blanket and some extra water and food, in case I need to work the entire night trying to extract a root.

The hours of this day stroll along and the warmest part of the afternoon has passed. I have already eaten and am thinking about going home when I see the root, barely hiding, almost waving at me.

How many times have I been on this path this year, in my life, and missed it? Much of the growth on the forest's floor has begun to die, as well as the red berries of the ginseng plant; they have fallen, making the plant more difficult to see. I stand back, as I always do when I find a root, but I am judging the weather and the amount of time left in the day. Not enough. The older the root, the wiser the root, the longer to remove it, the greater the care needed to do so. I go about preparing the area; first for the root, then for my night's stay.

How am I to sleep on this night? All these years I've dreamt of this day, a root such as this. Dreams that are not only mine but my father's and uncle's. How many generations back, I do not know. And here it is, only a sunrise away. As I lie awake, through the bending redwood branches I peer at the stars, but it is impossible to watch any one star or constellation as they seem to blink on and off between the moving boughs. This high in the mountains, the forest is already preparing for winter and constantly wakes me up: pine cones fall with a dull thud, crickets jump across the crisp leaves. If I listen closely, I can hear the trees slip out of their coats, preparing for a dormant six months of winter. I can't see the plant, but like a person's spirit, I know it is there.

The night descended on the mountain in a sprint. But now it dodders by.

The morning has come and I look at the root, which has been on this earth longer than I. This is the kind of root that can buy a hunter a house, that can provide for him for five or six years.

Extracting the great root, I follow the same routine as I would with a younger one—using the small spade to outline and dig the circle around the plant, but at a much slower pace. I study the root after removing each spade of soil, and as I draw closer to it, exposing parts of its legs, I put my mouth to the soil and taste it—the gritty and soft mixture of ancient minerals. In this moment, the world has shrunk to an eight-foot square; I don't acknowledge the ache in my calves or the knot in my lower back.

The legs of the root are beautiful, each of them thick as a finger; the beard is speckled with pearly spots. My nose touches the root and inhales its strong, bitter odor; only after boiling will a sweetness become its equal.

I am working with my hands when I hit a stone, not all that large, the size of a small potato. Part of the beard is wedged between the stone and a massive root of a redwood. I return to the spade, trying to free the beard, twisting and lifting until I can see how entangled it is. I hold the spade steady; my left hand is down in the soil, millimeter by millimeter freeing it. I am almost done when a shadow falls over me, clouds perhaps, although their shadows rarely penetrate the forest canopy. The shadow darts to the side and in an instant the spade slips, severing the delicate beard. The beard is free, but it is not supposed to be. Not this way. Part of it is in my hand, the rest is still caught between the rock and the tree. A man with a face as dirty as a charcoal maker's is on the path. A rush of fear hits me.

The dirty-faced man disappears as quickly as the value of the three-generation-old root. I stuff the severed root into my backpack and hurry down the mountain. If I had known the day would turn out this way, I would have stayed at home. Today will surely define the rest of my life as much as the killing of the sparrows defined my father's.

I admire their stalks, straight and a foot taller than I, three or four ears on each. From the front, their rows absorb me; the farther back they go, I have the illusion of their merging with one another. At least it has been a good year for the corn. A winter of corn bread and gruel awaits me.

I move through the field. About halfway past the twentieth row, I see a figure in the area where I have noticed some corn missing over the past couple weeks. Parting the rows, I realize that the person isn't standing but lying down.

I pause and analyze my position—as if I am hunting—from which direction should I approach the body? I enter the row almost on tiptoe. When I am within fifteen feet, I can see that it is only a girl, curled up asleep. I hold my breath, go down on my knees, and duck below the leaves.

Her matted, coiled hair has patches missing; her feet are thick, rotted black; her clothing is in bits and pieces. The girl's breathing is clogged, and several ears of corn are beside her. I think of what my lover told me on our first walk together, how they may look only ten years old but be sixteen. Taking that into account, I judge her to be no more than ten, as she looks about six.

I crawl closer, extend my arm to touch her; I am so close that I can see lice leaping in her hair and on her clothes. My hand is inches from her shoulder when one of the stalks, blown by the autumn wind, hits me on the head. I jump. What would I have said if she had awakened? I can't remember the last time I spoke to a child or was even near to one. I back up and leave the field, shoving aside the stalks.

My house is but fifty steps away; I am inside gathering bags of cornmeal, flour, sunflower seeds. But then I realize that the girl would never be able to carry everything across the river, so I remove some of the food from the basket. Still, there is too much. However, if I give her all of this, perhaps she won't return.

In the place where she was sleeping, I can see the indentation in the soil where she lay. With the basket in hand, I hurry down the row to the riverbank. No one. I scan the river. Nothing. But then I see her in the middle of the river. The water is at its lowest, reaching only her waist. She has taken off her blouse and is holding it above her head. It isn't until an ear of corn falls out of her blouse that I see what she is doing. She nearly slips while trying to recover the ear of corn, which the river has swiped from her; in doing so, she drops several more. The girl continues on toward the opposite bank and into the reeds. Soon she reappears and a soldier is waiting for her. I hadn't spotted him before, so engrossed was I in the girl. The soldier picks through the corn and sends her off. How many ears did he leave her? I stand watching until both of them disappear—the girl into the frontier and the soldier into his foxhole.

I go back to the field and set the basket down just in

case she returns. As I come near the house, the ducks gather and I empty my pockets for them. I know they too will soon leave.

Today I can't help but feel a tinge of resentment for this border, for how it has seeped into my life and begun to curdle. Like crossing the Tumen, here I am crossing back and forth over Miss Wong's offer.

I pass up a ride from the trucker and walk the eight hours to Yanji to give myself more time to consider the offer.

For the most part I have always made decisions promptly, but the truth is, the vast number of those decisions were forced by nature: the weather, the seasons, the ginseng growth patterns. If I were to bring her back with me and keep her safe, would it justify the price I paid?

I am at the door of the hotel once again, without an answer.

WHEN THEY take her to the reeducation camp, sunless days become nights without moons. Indoors, under lamps hotter than any star, they sing in praise of His Greatness. She competes with the others in the camp, seeing who can heap the most praise on Him. The title of the Dear Leader is no longer enough. Dear Dear Leader. Dearest of Dear Leaders. The Dearest Leader, son of the Greatest Leader. The titles grow more elaborate. Days and nights of building skyscrapers of praise.

She works in the camp, thousands of them work together to the hymn of praise; the swoop of a hoe, the scrape of a rake, the slamming of a sledgehammer, all in exaltation of the Dear Leader. At night she returns to her reeducation lessons. Even when the man is shot for stealing a guard's leather whip, chewing it as though it were food, the symphony doesn't stop; there is no pause in the cicada-like drone. The words become her breakfast, her sips of water, her pillow in the brief moments of sleep.

In her third and last week at the camp she is assigned to help raise the rabbits. They are cared for and fed much better than she is, she thinks. The temptation to sneak a leaf of cabbage or a mouthful of corn is great, but she reminds herself over and over that they murdered the man who stole the leather whip. Before she is released, many of the rabbits are killed and skinned; the skins are cleaned and sewn into the winter jackets for the soldiers.

The day she is set free, she walks the many miles home and finds her daughter in still worse condition. She is thinner and more disoriented, and her eyes are glazed over. But she is alive.

The load of branches rubs her neck and shoulders raw. She used to stop and rest, setting the pile of wood down and placing her head on it; several times she fell asleep this way. Not long ago, however, a group of boys came and pulled the wood out from under her and ran off with it. That is why she doesn't stop today.

The land levels off and her village comes into sight. A single crooked limb of smoke rises in the distance. Soon she is in front of the cracked white walls of the village's entrance. A man groans while pulling a cart of rocks; up ahead a woman lies on the dusty street, her arms bent in awkward angles. She wants to stop, something tells her to, but the weight of the wood keeps her moving. But she must go back and decides to retrace her steps. Looking at the woman's face, she recognizes her daughter's teacher, the one she fought with over the mugwort. She leaves the wood behind and goes after the man she just passed.

"Sir, I need your help."

"Help?"

"A woman is lying back there. I need to bring her to my house."

The man seems as if he will fall asleep, right there, on his feet.

"Please."

"It will be night soon," he says, nodding to where the sun has crept behind the mountains.

She despises him, knowing that although he will not ask, he will force her to say it.

"I will give you all of the wood that I have collected today."

She turns and starts back to the village.

"You carry the wood," he tells her.

He drags the teacher by the arms and places her on the rocks in his cart. The man is almost on both knees trying to move the cart; several stones spill over the sides. The teacher's hands dangle and bounce to the choppy rhythm of the man's steps.

"Go left at the next alley," she says to him.

The turn makes the man moan. She takes the bundle from her shoulders so that she can pass through the narrow alley; she follows the cart, holding the teacher's left foot, preventing it from scraping the sides of the houses.

"Stop. This is it."

She opens the door to the house abandoned by her neighbors long ago.

"Take her feet," he tells her.

The man grabs the teacher under the arms; she has her feet. The weight surprises her and she drops the teacher's legs to the ground. The man pulls the teacher into the house, lays her on the floor, face up, and without saying a word, he leaves.

It was only a couple of years earlier that her daughter and she would go to the edge of the village and wait for the garbage man and his oxen cart. The driver would sit high above them on his cart, and her daughter would laugh out in glee when he would jump off and land so softly that he hardly kicked up any dust. He would then lift the flap of his jacket pocket—the Dear Leader pinned to it—and pull out, like magic, a cracker or a piece of candy. But now the alleyway, like the whole village, smells of death; only the flies are thriving.

They have spent a night without a fire; it is cold on this morning when she hears the oxen cart. She goes outside, but her daughter remains in the house, and the driver gets down from his cart. Today no magic emerges from his jacket pocket. She struggles to pull the teacher outside, and the driver helps her; the back of the cart is already filled with the bodies of a man and a child. Unlike them, the teacher has clothes.

And this is when she sees the badge and wants to reach into the cart, grab it, and run back to the house. Maybe her daughter and she can somehow move away from this village. She knows of a village—Kachon—where a cousin of her husband lives. Maybe they could go there. She follows the man to the front of the cart.

"Where will you take her?"

"There's a pit near the mountain."

"Can I go with you?"

He offers his hand—it is warm and rough—and sits beside him; he gives her the stick and twice she strikes the red-brown ox. The sound of the ox's hoofs fills some of the quiet, but she can't take her mind off the badge lying in

100

the bed of the cart. She keeps her eyes on the bony flanks of the ox. The distance is much shorter than on foot and soon they are at the base of the mountain. The man takes the body of the small child—a boy, she notices for the first time, younger than her daughter.

Standing up on the cart, she peers into the pit. The old man gives the boy a shove and she watches him tumble and then settle among the other bodies. So many bodies down there; the stench nearly brings her to the ground.

She thinks about how she learned to bury corpses in the reeducation camp. Before throwing the dirt on the bodies, she had to take off their clothes and separate them into piles: shoes, tops, bottoms. That horrified her at first, but in time it became routine. The clothes and the blankets of the dead kept her and her fellow prisoners warm. And when she didn't dig the graves fast enough she was forced to squat for hours. But that was nothing compared to the sleep deprivation. Each time she would close her eyes and fall into a light sleep she would be awakened, only so that she could crawl back into another minute of sleep, over and over.

Next to the foot of the naked man lies the badge of the Great Leader. As the driver drags the dead man from the cart she jumps into the bed and snatches the badge. She tries to pin it on her shirt but her nerves won't allow it, so she closes her hand around it and goes to the lip of the pit. The dead man's body, the boy's father, she thinks, rolls less smoothly down into the pit and settles away from the boy's; she wishes the driver would climb in and move them closer together.

"Do you want her clothes?"

She doesn't understand what he is saying.

"The woman's clothes?"

"No, leave them."

The teacher's puffed ankles are soft, like bean curd, and she is afraid her fingers will puncture them. Her left hand is tight around the badge. They place the teacher at the edge of the pit and the man walks away, leaving her to push the body in.

THE DIM light is on, as it always is. I hear her crawl out of bed and I open my eyes slightly. The small vial of rat poison is in her hand and she is looking at it. I wish I were the kind of person who could reach out to her and tell her that everything will change. But I know I will never be like that.

It is early morning and I look for a piece of paper and a pencil. She has asked me to draw a map of the area for her. I abide by her wish, although I am not certain I can do this. I am barely familiar with more than a slice of this region.

The bends of the river near my farm and the mountains I know intimately. I use my memory of old maps that I have seen to sketch the downriver area. I know for certain that the Tumen River turns abruptly eastward, and then southward past the city of Tumen. From there, after about sixty miles, it empties into the sea near the point where China, North Korea, and Russia converge. I also know that there is a train that runs between Yanji and Tumen, although I have never been on it.

As I pencil in the altitudes of some mountains in the Nangang range, she asks how I know how high they are. I tell her that my uncle taught me, years ago. When I finish, I slide the map across the bed to her and she studies it, turning it in all directions. A damaged finger traces the course of the river, stopping at the various bends. I tell her that the small dotted lines, which fan out from my farm, indicate footpaths into the mountains, along the river and to Yanji.

She points to the name of Kaishantun. I explain that it is a filthy industrial town where the polluting of the river begins.

"That is where I crossed," she says and takes the pencil and writes the name *Sambong* on the map across the river from Kaishantun. Then, she writes the word *Namyang* across from the Chinese city of Tumen.

"How far is it from Yanji to Kaishantun?"

"More than a seven-hour walk."

"How many miles?"

"About fifteen."

"Is it mountainous?"

"Not so many mountains, but the dirt road is just a dried riverbed that becomes impassable in winter and in spring."

"Thank you for the map."

She folds it in half and in half again and puts it on the small table next to the lamp.

We enter Victory Park, passing Chairman Mao, who towers over us and all those doing tai chi. Every time I see a Mao statue, I can't but help think of the sparrows.

The morning is early and cool; slouched pines are blotched with frost; the sun has yet to burn off the hood of fog. All over the park the leaves are tightening and floating to their fallow graves.

I didn't sleep last night. No nightmares kept me awake,

only her words and the constant reminder that today I must tell her that I will not accept the proprietress's offer.

She is looking at the old men with their wooden bird-cages, chatting together as they most likely do every morning, as they have done for decades, for generations.

"What do they do with those birds?"

"I don't know."

"Maybe they are pets."

We move along, passing people who are stretching, others swatting shuttlecocks, some bellowing out songs, before coming upon a cluster of large swan paddleboats sitting still on the small lake.

"Have you ever been here?"

"Several times." Her answer surprises me.

I want to ask with whom, but stub out the urge to do so; instead I ask her this, my words sharper than I intend: "Is there nothing happy in your life?"

She continues along the path before suddenly turning to me.

"Catching snowflakes on my eyelids and seeing how they stay there for a short while and fracture the light into a prism of colors, then melt away, like tears sometimes melt away sadness." She stares up into a tree. "And you?"

I cannot answer.

I know that our time together is dwindling and I am confused by my desire. When we are together, I want to say: *Come back with me. Come back and share the winter and be there in the spring when I return from a day's hunting.* Yet when I am away from her, the solitude enfolds me. I am certain that the long, arduous winter will rub away my aching for her.

"I have never asked you your name."

She gives me none. We dig into our silences. How could I marry someone whose name I don't even know? I can see this is not the time to say anything about the proprietress's offer, which leaves me with a sense of relief at the sudden freedom this knowledge has given me.

I want this walk to end; I want to pick up my provisions and then be off. A falling leaf is caught on her left shoulder and teeters there until she shrugs it to the ground. I pick it up and carry it with me the rest of the way through the park.

Almost at this end of the park, to my surprise, we come upon an amusement park, a ghost town, void of people and working rides.

The top chair of the Ferris wheel creaks slightly in the northern breeze; I follow its hypnotic creaking. She steps over a low, rusty fence, goes and sits inside a tea cup and saucer, which are in dire need of a new skin. I sit down in the tea cup opposite her, and the longer we sit there the more I wish that this ride would come to life and spin us around like it is supposed to do. Spin and spin, hurling us both as far away from each other as possible.

From fifty yards away I see her sitting in the front of my house. And next to her lies a duck's white feather. It is so pure against her swollen black feet.

"Hello," I say, feeling unsure.

She squints as though the sun is setting behind me, but it is just past its apex and diminished by the clouds.

I don't move. I have no idea what to do next, I have no model. There are no children running around; they have left to the cities long ago. The valley is ancient. I am one of the youngest people for miles around, but right now, standing in front of this child, I too feel old.

"Hello," she quietly echoes my single word. I take several cautious steps toward her as though I am the visitor. I watch her struggle to her feet. She is so tiny; her brown eyes are enormous. Chestnuts. She has my lover's eyes. Her clothes hang as frail as a snake skin, one that has been shed and dried for days in the sun. Her right hand holds an unpeeled ear of corn. My corn. She has stopped squinting. Noticing me staring at the ear of corn, she shows no sign of guilt.

I fidget, trying to ease my nerves.

"I will make you something to eat."

As I push open the door, the girl takes hold of my arm. Startled, I nearly push her hand away. A bird claw. It is one of the neediest touches I have ever felt. I recall my lover's first touch and how it too begged for help. I realize that is what drew her to me.

I point her to the *kang*, near the stove, and add some kindling to the coals.

"I will make something to eat," I tell her, repeating what I said moments earlier.

In the kitchen I open the storage box, take out some

corn porridge, and place it into a pan on top of the stove. In a short time, the porridge is heated through.

The spoon looks like a ladle in her hand; I notice the effort it takes for her to lift it, but I have no other spoons. Every time my eyes look at her hideous feet, I think of my lover's fingertips. While I finish my porridge and corn bread, she manages to eat only a quarter of the porridge. She puts the bowl on the *kang* beside her and curls up, hugging the ear of corn, just as she was when I saw her in my field.

I take my dishes into the kitchen and go into the back room, returning with some blankets. Although it is only mid-afternoon, she is already asleep.

Her voice and a crunching sound are what wake me from a restless sleep, and I am lost in my own house. I don't move, allowing a lifetime of familiarity to tell me where I am. I slowly recall to whom the voice belongs. Who is she talking to? The late-night stove emits a soft umbra and by its light, ten yards away, I study her.

Close to her face, she holds the corn, which is still dressed in its husk and tassel of hair; she talks to it, not loud enough for me to understand what she is saying. The moment holds the intimacy of a mother and child. She nibbles on what appears to be an acorn, all the while talking to her corn doll. Watching, I feel less pity for her, maybe because in the low light those chestnut eyes are a little less haunting.

With the corn in hand, she gets up and walks toward

the door but is knocked to the floor by a support post in the middle of the room.

"Are you okay?"

I see a thin creek of blood creep down the side of her face and rush to the kitchen for a cloth and a bucket of water. I wring the cloth out and give it to her. She holds it against her head. The cut is not deep.

"What happened?"

"Sometimes I can't see."

"Is it too dark in here?"

"No. My mother told me it was because of eating rice root."

"Your mother?"

"Yes."

"Where is your mother?"

"I'm not sure. I think they took her away on the death cart. I haven't seen her for a long time."

She stares at me. I think that maybe her eyesight has returned, but I'm not certain. I take and rinse the cloth and put more wood into the stove.

"Can you see now?"

"It's better. I want to go back to sleep."

"Are you sure you're all right?"

"I'm tired."

I lie here. The girl's words about her mother bring to mind my lover. I know that I must go and see her soon.

THE NEXT morning they leave, carrying the framed picture of the Great Leader, the mining helmet, and the bread someone in the village has left for her daughter. They walk away from the sun, wearing all the clothing they own, a few layers beneath their coats.

They shove their way onto the train; the bodies pressed up against them do little to fight off the January cold. Her feet are the coldest, like she is wearing blocks of ice, but she notices that there are others who have no shoes at all. A strange image comes to her: scores upon scores of toes covering the floor, snapped off like frozen reeds.

There are electric outages and searches by the police; the train stops more than it moves. Many times the police scrutinize IDs. Some people are physically thrown off the train if their ID doesn't permit them to be in the region through which they are passing. Lately the punishment for not having a permit has been much harsher. After each check, she works a piece of bread, tucked under her jacket, into her sleeve, so that it drops down into her daughter's hand. She squeezes the small hand tightly to alert her daughter that the bread is there. As she has told her to do, her daughter goes to her knees and stays there until she has swallowed the last bite. Sometimes she manages to eat the entire piece, but it is difficult to do so without being seen. They have had to stand since they boarded. She wants to save the rest of the bread for her daughter, but she also fears the soldiers, knowing that if they find it they will take what little she has.

Too exhausted to keep standing, her daughter drops to the floor, letting go of her mother's hand. The train shifts. She lifts her daughter up, pleading with her to hang on to her leg.

There are many tunnels and they have just emerged from one; the gray light allows shapes to reappear. Nearby, a bite of rice drops to the floor; her daughter dives for the rice. She yanks her little girl's arm and pulls her to her feet. A soldier leers at her. She looks back to the floor. The rice is gone; a man on all fours has eaten it. A dull crack—like an ax brought down on a winter tree—and the man is flat on the floor.

"Next time wear your badge of the Great Leader on your coat so that everyone can see it."

She takes her left hand and touches her own badge, making sure it is straight; then she does the same with her daughter's.

Worse than the train is the donkey cart; the driver is hauling tree branches under which she and her daughter hide, having bartered their winter coats and half of the stone-hard bread. Every bump along the way jolts them, the branches spear them everywhere. From time to time, the driver stops and takes a brief nap under the cart. She taps on the floor of the cart and speaks to him.

"Is there food near the border?"

He responds with what she already knows. "Two autumns ago we had a flood and this past summer we had almost no rain."

"Are there rations?"

"Not in four years. Firewood is an even bigger problem. I can't take you much farther; I'm not permitted past the crossroads up ahead. The village you are looking for is through this valley, and over that mountain. Once you clear the mountain, it is about another sixteen miles. There will be an army barracks and a detention camp off to the north, you'll want to avoid them, stay as far to the south as you can; backtrack if you have to."

The man stops the cart and she thanks him. The donkey cart with the wood and their coats trundles away. Her daughter, wearing her father's mining helmet over a towel on her head, asks, "Is he a grape?"

"Yes, he is a grape."

And with that, they continue on foot, walking along the highway that the man instructed them to follow. She stares at the snow billowing across the pavement and refuses to look at the mountain up ahead, which doesn't seem to budge no matter how many steps they take.

She watches her daughter adjust the helmet, which keeps slipping off her head; every time the child touches it, her small fingers stick to the metal. They stop and she removes the towel from under the helmet and ties it over the top. This helps to keep it from sliding on her daughter's head.

They travel at night; when the new day appears she can

tell that they have finally made some progress. Two nights on the highway and nothing has passed them in either direction.

By the third day, they have made it up and over the mountain. Just as the driver had said, they see the army barracks and the camp, an enormous place, much larger than the camp she was in. It is a country unto itself.

Once they reach the bottom of the mountain, south of the camp, they rest in a grove of pines and are warmed by the fallen brown needles. She sleeps deeply, as does her daughter, both of them warmer than they have been in months. Before they leave, she buries beneath the needles the picture of the Great Leader.

Another day and night passes before they arrive in the village. The cousin they look for has been gone for years; his house lies abandoned like so many others.

"What happened to him?" she asks a lady.

The woman turns away, avoiding having to answer.

"Can we stay there?"

Again, no answer.

She tells her daughter to take two well-folded bills from her pocket; she holds them up in front of the lady.

"Can we stay there?"

"It's not in good condition, but it has a roof. It's the sixth house down the fifth lane to the left."

"Where are all the people?"

The woman is quiet, but as they start walking she responds, "In a grave or across the river. The only two places we can go."

She understands now that their time here will be very short—until the village spies catch up to them.

Just as she predicted, in less than a week, a group of men come and carry her away. She thinks she is being taken to the massive reeducation camp they passed, but she can't be certain because they tie a sack around her head, keeping her moving, sometimes in a vehicle, sometimes on foot. She never sees her daughter again.

I HAVE two bowls of kerosene and I set them on the floor, one on each side of the girl. "You must clean your head with this. Put your fingers into the bowl on the right, and then rub your head with the kerosene. This will kill the lice. Clean your fingers in the other bowl."

Before I leave her alone, I tell her that it might hurt.

I remember how my mother shaved my head in summer to help make the lice easy to find as well as to keep them away. My father taught me about using kerosene, and as a boy I cleaned the goats this way. The goats bleated as I did this, but as the girl dips her fingers into the bowl and rubs her scalp, she doesn't make a sound.

I go and open the blue-shuttered window at the opposite end of the room. Spangles of afternoon sun splinter onto the floor. I glance back at the girl and try to imagine her in a school uniform, like the one my lover told me about when she was a young girl:

It is my first day. The starched blouse makes my arms itch. I don't move and the teacher motions for me to walk between the two rows of the oldest students—the fourth graders—who are waiting on the school grounds. I hesitate, but start to move forward with a step, then another. At the front of the rows, a shower of colorful, small pieces of paper rain down upon me. I walk and the paper continues to pour, sticking to my short black hair, the sleeves of my rice-white blouse, my blue skirt, the red handkerchief tucked into my pocket.

The girl is still cleaning her head with the kerosene; I am lulled by the repetition of the movements of her hands. I turn to look out the window again. When she has finished, I take the bowls of kerosene out and dump them behind the shed. Away from her I can think more clearly about what I must do. She needs a bath and I must find her some clothing; these simple necessities I understand. I suddenly see the girl, hobbling toward the river.

I take off after her; she is easy to catch. Some of the corn that she has in her arms drops to the ground. I look across the river and check to see if there are any soldiers out along the banks; there is no one.

Not until we are back in the house and the door is latched do I speak to her.

"You can't go outside. You can't be seen over here."

"I must give the soldiers their corn."

"It is too dangerous to keep crossing the river."

"If I don't give them the corn, they will come for me."

"No one will come here." I want to sound convincing. "You must not leave the house."

She looks at me and I think she is about to cry. I pull the iron tub to the center of the room, close to the stove; I have started to heat a large pot of water.

She watches as I prepare the bath. As I heat more water, I search for some clothes for her. An impossible task in this house. It's been more than a decade since that disastrous winter when the woman came to stay. I find a pair of cotton trousers and a jacket. I cut the legs and sleeves to about the girl's length and cut the leftover pieces of sleeves into two long, thin strips, making them into belts: one for the jacket and one for the trousers.

"You can wear these until I find something your size."

Her silence makes me uncomfortable. She is looking at the wall beyond me; much like my lover, she has disappeared into her thoughts. At this moment, I admit to myself what I have so foolishly been denying: I can't do this alone. There is no other way but to go to Yanji, buy my lover from Miss Wong, and bring her back—once again, allowing a woman into this house. Only she can help.

I see the tub, a cap of steam rising from it.

"I will go outside while you bathe," I say. "There is soap and a towel, and you can put on those clothes."

I hear the splash as she enters the bath and remember how bad I felt when my mother scolded me the day I dug up the garden looking for the painted ants. Maybe that is how the girl is feeling since I spoke so sternly.

Looking at the shed, I think it can be fixed up without too much work; it would give us some extra space to live. This thought gives me a sense of having some control over what is happening. The two of them could live in the shed, leaving me alone in the house.

The late afternoon light dissolves and speaks of the onset of winter, which this year is later than usual. A few stubborn leaves, their sap already drained from them, clutch the branches.

Tonight she eats more than she did in the previous days. As she eats, her corn doll rests in the left pocket of the cotton jacket. She has tied one of my red ginseng-hunting cloths around her head. I gave her some aloe and crushed medicinal herbs to rub on her feet, which she has wrapped in towels. I feel as though I can breathe a little now as I become more comfortable with her in the house.

"How much corn do the soldiers take from you?"

"The nice soldier takes only half, the other one takes more, sometimes all of it. He's the one with my badge."

"What badge?"

"Of the Great Leader."

"Why does he take your badge?"

"Without it my life is not complete, without it I can be arrested. He holds it for me until I come back, and each time I give him the corn he returns the badge. He even cleans it for me, because I was bad and got it dirty."

"Tomorrow I will buy you a new badge of the Dear Leader."

"The Great Leader," she corrects me.

"What?"

"The badge is of the Great Leader."

Just like when my lover talks of them, I am confused as to who is who.

"How can you find me a new badge?" she asks.

"They sell them in the city. Tomorrow morning I must go there."

The fire in the stove crackles. Two logs warm me from three body lengths away. Soon, I know, I will have to move closer and closer to the stove in order to draw the same amount of warmth from those two logs. The heated platform *kang* is the best place in the house; its bricks can hold the heat for hours. Now, the girl sits there.

"Where are you from?"

"My village is over the mountains, but I haven't been there in a long time."

"Where have you been staying?"

"Sometimes I sleep in a village. There are a lot of empty houses. The train station is also a good place, but there are so many people, and some of them try to steal my corn."

"You must stay here until I return. I will be back maybe tomorrow night or early the following day, but you cannot leave the house."

There is doubt in her eyes. I wonder what she sees in mine.

In the middle of the "ten days of death" I set out for Yanji. It was my father who gave that name to this time of year, the only time when this valley is stagnant; the time before the first snow, when the valley smells like cold steel, when the elms, the birches, the oaks have dropped the last of their leaves from their arthritic fingers, when even the winds are resting, preparing for the months of labor that are ahead.

There is no ride this morning and I walk more than halfway before a man with a horse-drawn cart offers to take me the final miles to the eastern ridge of the city.

In Yanji, high above the valley, it is more bitter than when I left home in the early hours. There is already a dusting of snow, which swirls with each step I take.

On my way to the hotel, I buy two badges: one of the Great Leader, the other of his son, the Dear Leader. The girl can have whichever one she wants, or both of them.

The lobby of the hotel is warm, the smell of heating oil permeates the air. On a chair, cradling my cup of tea, I wait for my fingers to come back to life. I have yet to see the proprietress; a different woman serves me the tea and tells me a room will soon be ready. I wonder if the proprietress is not here, or whether she keeps from showing herself because of her dissatisfaction with my indecisiveness. After I tell my lover of the plan to bring her back to my farm, I will talk with Miss Wong and negotiate a price.

I am told to go to my room on the third floor. I've been walking up these steps for thirty years. I think how I will tell her about the girl, tell her that I want to buy her. Buy her. The words clot in my throat. The hallway, as always, is musty.

A woman sits on the corner of the bed, the top blanket already folded down. I check the number on the door. I think of my father's words: how so many things can be accomplished in ten days. I know how much can also be wasted. I force myself to look at the woman on the bed. Is my lover brightening another room?

Sharply I close the door; my resentment surfaces.

"Where is the other woman?"

"What woman?"

"The North Korean one who's usually in this room."

"There is no one here from that country."

"I have seen her regularly for six months and I have

spoken with the proprietress about her. Miss Wong knows who she is. She knows she is the only one I want to see."

"No North Koreans are permitted to work here," she answers tersely.

I decide to stay in hopes of finding out as much information as I can. I also realize that finding a ride this late in the day would be nearly impossible, and a walk through most of the night is not inviting. The girl will be okay, I think; the house is full of food and firewood.

Where could she have gone? Is she on her way to South Korea? Or did Miss Wong sell her to another man or, worst, turn her over to the police?

During the night there aren't enough blankets in the entire hotel to warm me, so I pull the top blanket from the bed, wrap myself in it, and tread out into the hallway. Without shoes, I feel the scars of cigarette burns on the carpet. At each door I stop, lean in, and listen for a hint of my lover's voice, her breathing. Door by door. Nothing. Nothing. Down to the second floor. Nothing.

Back in the room, the woman is asleep, not even aware that I had left. I untangle myself from the blanket, stand naked and cold, then put on my clothes, grab my knapsack, and close the door behind me. Again I pause at each door, both on this floor and the one below, and listen. I take the back stairway down to the lobby.

The same woman who served me tea rises from her chair, but before she's able to say anything I demand to see Miss Wong.

"She isn't here."

"She must be. I will wait until she agrees to speak with me." I sit down in a chair.

The woman hesitates, then disappears into a room off the lobby. Shortly, Miss Wong comes out.

"Why wasn't I given my lover tonight? You know that it is only she who I want to see."

"She is not your lover. I gave you a chance, several months ago, to claim her. You never responded to my offer."

"Now I am ready."

"It is too late. She is no longer with us."

"What do you mean?"

"There is nothing more to say. I must ask you to leave now."

I open the door, and into the calm late night I walk, colder than when I entered.

At the market, before dawn, I find a truck hauling vegetables and I am given a ride to the city of Tumen. The thirty-one miles, following the river, is the farthest I have ever been from my farm. She spoke about the city of Tumen and about what happens there on Fridays. Today, I go to find her. I imagine she may have come here, and need to find out for my own satisfaction or, maybe, to ease my mind.

I am dropped off alongside the railroad tracks and follow them until they lead onto a trestle over the river. I can see two soldiers, one in green uniform, the other in brown, guarding opposite ends of the trestle. The truck driver told me that once there was a time when trains crossed the river with passengers headed to South Korea from the Soviet Union. Years since that has happened. Still, the sentries man the tracks as if at any moment one of those steam ghosts will rumble on by.

I continue along the tarmac road. I find a small park along the river where, on this cloudy late November morning, I can sit on a bench within view of Tumen Bridge, the only official border crossing for many miles. It is midmorning, and I finally hear a truck, a large flatbed with a wooden fence about five-feet high on all sides. She told me this truck comes through here nearly every day, but always on Fridays.

Faces peer over the truck's fence; from between the lower slats eyes of children and teens stare. The truck has stopped at a traffic signal. I look for her and run around to the other side, but it is difficult to see inside and there are so many people in there. Every generation has its swallows, it seems, swallows that eat the grain from our fields and then are gone.

As I am about to cross back to the other side of the street, a soldier stops me.

"What are you doing?"

"Looking for someone."

"Get away from the truck."

I return to my park bench and watch them unload the people from the truck. There is no one I know, but one after the other they start to look familiar. They are quiet and don't resist. Only one woman is screaming, digging her heels into the ground, but she isn't much trouble for the guards who have her by the elbows and easily carry her toward the North Korean soldiers waiting at the bridge's midway point.

She spoke of Namyang, the small North Korean city directly across from where I stand; the empty truck is backing off the bridge now. She wrote the name of the place, in her language, on the map that I had drawn for her and told me how the people would be taken to the city square and humiliated and beaten and executed in front of the crowd, branding into the minds of those who watched that the river should not be crossed.

I try my best to listen for the sounds of the people. She told me, if I tried hard, I could hear them.

But I hear nothing.

I listen some more.

Are those their screams or only the caws of a crow? Time slides by and still nothing. Several kids nearby erupt in laughter and remind me where I am.

The driver of the vegetable truck said I would have no trouble finding a ride from Tumen south to Kaishantun. In an hour we have reached the outskirts of the industrial town, a little more than ten miles from home. From here, however, there is no more paved road, so I must walk the rest of the way to my farm. Into the mean-spirited wind, I follow the river westward, moving slowly.

Opposite, the frontier is on edge. A lone brown kite vacillates in the wind, stalking something to eat. Two soldiers are strengthening the roof of their foxhole. I am cold but try not to think about it, continuing my steady pace—one foot in front of the other. I mark the distance by the foxholes I pass: near the border towns, there are eleven or twelve foxholes every mile; away from the towns, only two or three.

I stop and seek out the support of a tree. A donkey dithers by; it stops and we look at each other. Across from me lies the town of Sechon, a hamlet it seems, barely big enough to scratch a mark on my map. Could this be the cousin's village she spoke of, so close to my farm? No, I don't think the name was Sechon but something like it.

Twenty-seven degrees, and across the way not a chimney speaks. The only sign of life is from a single weak bulb in a window of a pockmarked apartment building. Suddenly the sound of rapid gunfire shakes me from my daze and sends me diving into the brush. My embarrassment slowly coaxes me out. There are no bullets shredding my side of the frontier, only a loud, crackling voice: "Comrades, the Great Leader lives eternally in our hearts and the Dear Leader takes our great country into the twenty-first century."

I observe Sechon and wait for someone, something, to be stirred by the voice. I wait while the voice continues, hiccuping over and over the same words that inspire nothing. No chimney chokes up smoke, no ox or donkey or car resurrects itself in the streets, no single bare bulb flickers. In the foxhole, fifty yards away, the breaths of the soldiers are the only sign of life. Up in the middle of their mountain large white letters have been placed proclaiming: LONG LIVE THE SON OF THE 21ST CENTURY!

Again I think of her as I am nearing my farm. Winter is in pursuit and no matter how fast I walk, it will certainly catch me.

I can see the child isn't here. There are not many places for me to search. I go to the kitchen, then to the mound of firewood by the shed and to the harvested cornfield— although, with only its stubble left, the field is not much of a hiding place. I know that if she went back to North Korea, there is nothing I could do. My exhaustion dominates me.

Later, when I manage to shake off my sleep, I see the stack of corn on the floor. I am not sure how I could have missed it. When I looked for her, I would have had to walk by the corn at least twice. The pyramid starts at six and climbs all the way to one. A gift?

I go outside and come upon them in my scarred garden. They neither hide nor run. The three of us wait, imprisoned by the patch of land, trying to figure out the next move. You have your life to protect, the farmer told me.

"What do you want here?"

The skinny, frightened men turn to each other. One of them begins motioning with his hands to his mouth, as if eating. And then I realize I've seen this young man before. The same dirty face of the one who caused me to sever the great root. Once again, I am flushed with anger.

"I speak your language. What is it you want?"

Again, the sign language. I don't believe that they cannot speak.

"Is it food?"

They nod. If I feed them I know they will be like the stray cats that the truck driver spoke of.

"Did you see a girl here?"

They look at each other and then shake their heads no.

"She was in my house just yesterday. She is North Korean, like you."

"We want something to eat, that is all. It is cold up in the mountains." At last the dirty-faced man speaks.

"Did the soldiers come and take the girl?"

"We don't know anything about the girl."

"Tonight you stay in that shed."

I unlock the shed; they go inside, cautiously, like animals into a cage. I begin to lock the door, thinking of how the girl fled, and then I change my mind. You lock in only that which you wish to keep. Go if you want, please go.

In the front room of the house, the kindling and quartered logs are stacked December-high—ceiling to floor. The fire in the oven will not die for the next half year. The gruel is mushy and the wafts of chili peppers and salt settle into the notches of the room. They can probably smell it out there. I set aside a bowl for myself, take the large pot of gruel and spoons out to them. The men are huddled close together. I place the pan on the floor and notice for the first time that one of the men is without shoes.

"I will bring some blankets."

I leave, not waiting around to see if they pick through the food, looking, as my lover did, for shards of glass. On the way to the house, I see a piece of the cotton material on the ground; it's the belt I made for her. I do not trust them.

When I take the blankets out to the shed, I hold up the belt.

"This belongs to the girl."

The men look quickly at it, not denying or affirming what I just said. The man with the dirty face speaks once more.

"The girl was outside, down near the river, and we thought she would draw attention to us. We were afraid. Twice we have been returned, each time we have escaped. They will not hurt a little girl, but if they catch us, we will be killed."

"What did you do with her?"

The other man speaks.

"I told her that we were North Korean agents and that we would give her a chance to sneak back across the river, and if she didn't we would turn her over."

"But she is only a small girl. Winter is here and there is no food in your country. She will not survive the season."

"We have to come down off the mountain. There is already snow up there and we would not make it through the winter either."

"Why should I care? When did she leave?"

"Early in the morning, when it was still dark. I watched her; she made it safely across."

Safely to a place where she is not safe, I think.

The hue of the valley—its amber torso and crystal feet—is what I will recall most vividly about this night. The crystallization of the valley isn't a rare phenomenon, it happens every November. Just before the river freezes, the air carries within it a deep cold, and as the warmer water rises, its vapor latches onto anything—branches, harvested cornstalks, fences, the tops of roofs—until the valley is gripped by a transparent sheen. Tonight the divide between the sky and valley is so perfect, so well defined, that the land and sky are truly separate beings. When I close the door to my house, however, I know that my life has changed for good. I wake the men because I cannot let them stay any longer; they must not come here again. It would only be a matter of time before the soldiers would spot one of them.

I give them food, the food of a hunter, which they can easily eat while on the move: corn cakes and dried fruit. The path is level; its pale crust of gemlike frost crunches under the weight of each footstep. The wind chimes in the trees. I don't turn around to see if the two men have fallen behind. I burrow forward, not wanting to think about the one behind me without any shoes.

There is time for me to change course, turn back, go home, bar the door. Yet knowing that I was willing to take this enormous first step has already left me a different man.

Along this mountain trail it normally takes an hour without stopping.

"Stay here, until I return."

The men are obedient, never questioning my motives; they go into the frozen thicket to hide. Do I have any choice but to trust you? she once asked. The power in this is the responsibility.

The crossroads pointing to the cities of Yanji and Tu-men are a mile away, and, before coming up to the cluster of vehicles, I see that the truck is there. I talk to the driver. When we are finished, the driver rolls up the window and I walk the mile back to where I left the men; they haven't moved.

The truck is waiting near the mouth of the trail. Its window is less than a third of the way down and the driver stays in the cabin; the warmth inside drifts out and burns my face. The driver digs into his pocket, counts out the bills, folds them over once, and places four hundred *yuan* in my hand. I glance to see if the two men are watching; they are not. The window is rolled back up before I turn away.

"This man will help you," I tell the two men. Their expressions do not change. I unhook the door to the bed of the truck and nod to them.

If I look up into the sky it is difficult to see the flurries falling. If I could just catch one of the flakes on my lash, would I be able to see through her eyes something that made her happy?

WHEN IT comes to rivers, those that serve as boundaries are the most burdened rivers of all. And on this day, in the final month of the old century, there is no river carrying more troubles than this one.

The Tumen sloughs along, much of its voice lost during the night. The river singes aimless snowflakes. Near to its edges, the water becomes almost slush—the texture of overcooked rice. When a branch, weighted by ice, snaps from a tree and falls into the river, hardly a splash is left behind, instead a sucking sound, a whisper, as the branch gradually sinks into the river's depths. Spreading inward from its banks, the slush coagulates, hardens, ambushes leaves and twigs and leaves them to fossilize until spring, when the waters will carry them downstream in a steady procession of late-autumn relics.

WHEN THEY have enough use of her labor in the second reeducation camp, they beat her fingertips—not the whole of her hands, just the ten tips of her fingers. They use bars of metal, sticks with nails, pipes. They release her, and every time she touches something she is reminded that she is nothing more than a grape.

The days are not cold enough to numb the pain in her fingers, which are purple and red and, in places, a strange bluish-green. Almost beautiful, if they weren't so hideous. She thinks about her daughter and how she used to plait her hair, and knows she will never do so again.

The reeducation camp is near the border, she thinks. When she is released, it is still winter. All around the outskirts of the camp is a huge emptiness. She thinks she is going in the right direction toward her husband's cousin's village, but after walking for hours, there is not a shrub, a road, or even a mountain that she recognizes. Had she been taken somewhere else, to a different camp altogether?

The absence of the camp's incessant exaltation for the Dear Leader makes her feel as though she has gone deaf. Silence is the most imposing thing on the frontier. She tries pulling weeds with her wrists, because her hands are useless; she braces herself on her elbows and knees to eat.

The village where she left her daughter seems to have

vanished, as if an avalanche buried it. After days of searching, she begins to notice a warming in the air and she knows that she must attempt to cross the river, the river that she hears is the border. She has been told to cross it when it is still frozen. Spring would be too late.

THERE IS no moon; the stars are everywhere. I lie back and attempt to pick out the individual stars from the vast sheet of white that they appear to be. When I was a boy, my mother and I would go outside on nights such as this, each of us carrying a bench. We would lie down and watch the sky. She told me that this was the only way to truly see it. She was correct. After a while, it would be as if the sky and the earth were reversed. Turned upside down—like right and wrong, I think.

Tonight, however, it is much too cold to lie here for long. The clattering of cans detonates the night. I bolt upright on the bench. I can see the girl struggling to untangle her foot from the wire fence. I know it is her because of the clothes she wears.

I tell myself I must go down to the river, but instead I remain on the bench. The girl manages to free herself and takes several steps onto the frozen Tumen. She walks slowly and now I am up off the bench, running. I am about to shout for her to hurry, when a number of shots rip through the valley. The girl is lifted off her feet like a crane in flight, and just as quickly, she hits the ice and slides. The shots continue to reverberate. Her body finally comes to rest about fifty yards downriver. Suddenly I realize how exposed I am and rush to a group of trees along the bank. I know the soldiers have seen me. I grab a long stick and step out, shouting upriver:

"If you come out of the foxhole, I will shoot you."

I can't believe I have screamed this and only hope that

the hundred yards has blurred my attempt of brandishing a branch for a gun.

I keep close to the ground, narrowing the distance between the girl and me. Every ten yards I pause and look back upriver to see if the soldiers have come out of the foxhole. They have not, at least not as far as I can tell. There is no breeze; the girl's body doesn't move. I want to bring her back to the house. That must have been where she was headed.

I am flat on my stomach—swimming on ice. I try not to think. I reach the girl and again I scan the river. Nothing. Heat rises from her body and around her the ice is red. I extend my arm, like that day in the cornfield, but tonight I touch her shoulder and then lift her hair, which has nearly froze to her face. I close her eyes. She looks the same as she did when she was asleep in my house, just a small child with her childhood still intact. I have her in my arms, this time not bothering to stop and look. If the soldiers were to come, there is nothing I could do.

When I open the door, I feel the heat upon me and know I can't keep her in here. I take her to the shed where the temperature is almost as cold as outside. In the rear, there is a worktable that I rarely use; I lay her on it and cover her with a blanket.

When I finally leave the shed and return to my house, the heat from the stove has died, the coals have grown cold and turned to ash.

December's brittle frontier; the slightest touch could send a blade of grass tumbling into a weed crashing into a stalk of corn smashing into a tree, on and on, sending the whole of the valley into a wave of violent shivers, cleaving it apart.

I force myself outside on this day, as I have on most days since I locked the door of the shed. Within minutes, ice forms on the tundra of my face, and when I raise my eyebrows, flecks of frost fall from them.

I look out onto the river, searching for clues from that night. I expect to see her blood or her reflection in this mirror of ice. But there is nothing.

The air has begun to hurt my lungs and I turn to the south toward where I hear a chipping sound; there is a soldier kneeling on the river, pounding the ice again and again with the barrel of his rifle. Pieces of ice fling up into the air. The soldier collects them into small piles and then scoops them into a sack. He never looks my way, just continues to gather the ice. I move in the direction of the soldier, kicking loose a chunk of ice, bigger than my foot, that hangs from the lip of the bank; then I kick loose another. Now I am nearly across from the soldier, two dozen paces between us. I toss the first chunk of ice; the second one chases it, spiraling past the soldier.

The soldier eyes me and says nothing. Is he the one who shot her? I know that the soldier, with a lift of his rifle, a bend of his finger, could kill me. I know that no one would miss my absence. This is possibly the only thing I share with the girl. I toss around the vilest things to shout at him but can't find my courage, and I turn my back on him and on the river.

At the first knock on the door I think it is only the wind wanting in. Even when I hear a voice, I still can't believe there is someone here. When did I have a visitor last? Is it the soldier?

I open the door and standing there, in snowshoes, is the farmer. I recognize my neighbor not by his face, bundled entirely in a scarf, but by the way he leans to the left, which is more pronounced with all the clothes.

"Come in."

"Thank you." His voice lugs the winter inside. After removing his snowshoes, the man stands his rifle against the inside of the door.

"Go and sit on the *kang*. I'll make some ginseng tea."

"Thank you." Only the sounds of the flickering fire and wind fill the house; when one dies down, the other takes over, they are the two constants of winter. I spoon some honey into both cups of tea and hand one to the man.

Lowering the scarf from his face, he blows on the tea and sips it.

"Very good. How long have you been hunting?"

"My whole life. Even as a child, before I learned the trade, I would help my father and uncle dry and prepare the ginseng."

I wait for the man to finish his tea, knowing he isn't here to talk about hunting.

"I came out here because you helped me with my bull. As I told you then, things were going to become much worse. Last week, over in Baishin, a man and woman were robbed, tied up, and killed by some of those Koreans. And they did that after the couple had invited them to sit and eat with them."

"Were they caught?"

"No, and they never will be. How are you going to catch them? They're all over this place."

The man has unraveled his scarf; his hat lies on his lap. For the first time I can see his tangled head of hair.

"Do you have a gun?"

"No."

"With mountain lions and occasional tigers out here, you're putting yourself in danger. And now with all those people coming into our country, crossing over, you're even more at risk."

"The ginseng gods protect me."

I've never put much faith in it. Over the years, I had heard my uncle murmur this and I know some hunters today still live by it. Although I feel ridiculous saying it, it is simpler than telling him that I am scared of guns. I don't even know how to use one.

From under his parka, the man takes out a handgun and sets it on the floor with its grip facing me. I stare at it as if it were a viper and wonder if it will strike at me. He places a handful of bullets next to the gun.

"You know how to use one, don't you?"

"I'm not all that skilled, but I can manage," I lie. "Really, I don't need one. No one will disturb me here, especially now that it's winter."

"That's what the couple over in Baishin thought. What kind of animal kills the person who feeds him?"

What kind of person, I think, after feeding him turns around and sells him? Two banks to every river, each carrying a hundred different stories.

"You keep that gun, and when spring comes return it to me, and then go and buy yourself one."

"Thank you."

The man struggles to his feet and I hold out an arm and help him up.

"Winter's terrible on an old man's body."

"Wait, I'll prepare a bundle of food and some ginseng for you to take back."

"You don't have to do that."

"You came all the way here to talk to me."

I pack some honey, a couple of good roots of dried red ginseng, the warming kind for winter, fistfuls of beans and corn, and wrap them tightly together.

"You are welcome to stay the night."

"No, my wife is alone. I will be home in a couple of hours."

"Be careful."

"Don't worry about me. Anything that moves will have a bullet in it. Animal or man."

After putting on his snowshoes, the man grabs the rifle in one hand, the bundle in the other, and goes in the direction of the river. I am about to tell him to take the path that runs behind the house—it would cut nearly half an hour from his trip—but then I catch myself, realizing that the farmer would have to pass by the shed.

The days disappear along with the roots on the floor. The younger roots I dry and powder, and will sell them to buyers who will use them to make teas and vitamins. This is the part of the job, the only part, I don't like. I know, however, with fewer and fewer aged roots to be found, I am dependent on the money I make from younger roots. Yet none of this monotonous powdering of the root helps to soothe me.

On nights when I can't sleep, and there have been many of late, I grind more roots into powder. Soon the floor is bare, leaving me space to pace freely. Now my only priority is to keep the *kang* heated and the stove fed. Unlike the ginseng root on the floor, the stack of wood doesn't seem to change. Only after a week can I tell it's shrinking. If the fire dies again, winter will invade, take over the house, and be an unwanted occupier until summer.

The wind speaks from the other side of the valley, up from the southeast. I have on my snowshoes and lift the handle and hold on to it as I thrust my shoulder against the door. It edges open. The cold attacks me; the snow is ice. Off toward the river, I can barely make out the snowdrifts that are higher than the donkey I saw on the dirt road a couple of months ago. Today I wouldn't even be able to find a frozen gray ear sticking up through these drifts.

In all directions the terrain repeats itself: white on white, blasted by the winds. Only the tone varies, a touch of gray in the shade, pure, eye-stinging white in the sun. Somehow a group of black birch, the toughest of trees, has managed to escape the frigid bristles of January, producing a splotch of faded black against this white madness.

The shed is a half-minute walk away in the spring; ten

minutes in the winter. But the wind has carved out a makeshift path.

I unlock the shed's door and work on opening it, heating it with my breath until I am able to jar it free. The daylight enters with me. I remember my father and I building this shed when I was a boy still learning about ginseng hunting.

"A place for a man to think or forget. Everyone needs such a place," my father told me when we had completed it.

Inside there is not much clutter, although every year small things seem to move in here: extra tools, some corn, a chair in need of repair, and now the girl. She is covered by a quilt, made by a village woman, for which I bartered a season's worth of ginseng. There is no odor of decay; this is the best freezer in all of Changbai, I think, with a hint of pride.

I am not sure why I came out here, maybe it was only for the chance to be away from the house. I listen for the direction from which the wind is blowing. Even a one-hour shift in another direction could lock me inside here. Before this year, the thought that I would, in all likelihood, die alone, was comforting to me. Today, in here with the girl, the thought unnerves me. I reach out and unfold a quarter of the quilt to reveal her face. White with several blotches from scabs.

I lower another part of the quilt; her right arm cradles an ear of corn, which I placed there. Beneath the cotton jacket, I know, is the single hole in her chest, enormous and probably a brownish purple by now—like the inside of a deer antler when you cut it too short.

I cover the girl, giving her barely a final glance, and shut the door, taking the dim light with me.

The front door bursts inward and one of the soldiers has a rifle trained on my face less than a yard away. I recognize the soldier, the same one who was chipping the ice on the Tumen. Another soldier searches my house. I notice the badge on the soldier's jacket and try to remember whether the smiling man with glasses is the Great or the Dear Leader. I am interrupted, however, by a scalding pain in my left shoulder that sends me crashing into the soldier next to me. I recover my balance, but tears are in my eyes. I think of the handgun but it is on the woodpile without any bullets.

"The girl!"

"What girl?"

"We saw you take her."

"She's not here."

"What did you do with her?"

Fire erupts in my shoulder again. When a shot explodes through the side wall I go down on one knee. The barrel of the rifle is a cold circle against my temple. The smoke from the shot stings my nostrils and burns my eyes.

"The next bullet is for you. The girl!"

A sour churning in my stomach rises in my throat. I swallow.

I am on my feet, stepping over the broken door and outside. Snow has already intruded into the house. I am tempted to run, but I know I haven't a chance. In seconds the frigid air has pinned me.

I lead the soldiers to the shed and fumble with the lock; my fingers don't seem to work. Suddenly a bullet blows open the door. I remain outside. One soldier comes out with a sack of grain over his shoulder and points his rifle mockingly at me. The second one walks out with the girl. They walk away. I watch them until they appear to be one and I cannot tell which of them is carrying the girl.

The snow is more formidable in the direction of the river. Dunes of snow. Up and down I disappear into their cleavage. I bite at the mustache of ice on my lip, wait for the gun to go off in my pocket, ripping me to pieces. When it doesn't, I forge my way up and over the next dune. Finally I reach a plateau, high as the roof of my house; I find a firm spot and sit facing the river. Although I feel its weight in my coat pocket, I still check. I pull out the gun; its density surprises me even though it is not all that much bigger than a root. After the soldiers came for her, it took me many tense days to figure out how to load and unload the gun. For hours I gawked at it on the floor, tried to figure it out in my head; then suddenly I had it in my hands, and was analyzing the angles and curves. When I opened the chamber, I left it like that for long stretches of time. Then I took out the bullets, one at a time, placing them back in the chamber, taking them out again.

I hear an occasional crunching sound in the snow, possibly an animal or just the wind blowing a branch across the icy landscape.

The girl isn't the only reason that forces me out here

today. I think about the two men. I want to find someone to blame for my wrongdoings. Across the frozen river is a foxhole only a hundred yards away, easy for me to locate. I know where it is. I sit on the plateau and aim the gun at the foxhole, only a hundred yards away, and pull the trigger, and again, and again, three more times, again. Each click answers the previous, tossing a limp echo throughout the frontier. I would like to laugh at myself for leaving the bullets back in the house, but I can't seem to do so. I turn to go back, and there in front of me is a soldier, one of the ones who came for the girl. He has a rifle, which he has flung harmlessly over his shoulder.

"We are out of food."

I look and try to find myself in him, or my father or uncle. I don't. I think of what my lover told me about the soldiers, about their cruelty, but I don't see that in him either.

"How much food do you need?"

"For myself and another comrade."

"I will go to the house and bring you some."

"Bring it to the foxhole." He pauses, perhaps anticipating my apprehension. "You can slide it across the river to our bank. I will come out and get it."

It is difficult for me to get up from my crouching position. My body doesn't want to move. A body suddenly aged.

At the house I remove the snowshoes and stick the gun in the far corner on the stack of firewood, where I will not have to touch it until spring. I haul the wooden crate of food for the soldiers down to the border. I walk halfway out onto the river, directly across from the foxhole. This is the closest I have ever been. The foxhole looks larger than I expected, shabbier as well. Pieces of wood and reeds hang loosely from the edge of the roof. I don't see the soldiers, but I know that they are inside watching me. I set the crate on the ice and give it a push; it slides unobstructed toward its destination.

ONCE SHE has scaled the treacherous mountains, she must avoid the checkpoints since she has no papers permitting her to travel in the neighboring province, even though she is only twenty-five miles from her village. The days are without food and the snow she eats makes her stomach cramp. In the flatland of the valley, she moves around only at night. The final phases of the moon pass. Beneath a cloud-covered black sky she reaches the river. All that she has learned about the Tumen is rendered useless, because the width and depth and speed are cloaked in late winter. Perhaps she remembers skating on a frozen pond with her father, gripping his hand. She can only hope that what she has heard is true: that far away from the towns the soldiers are stationed in foxholes every five hundred yards instead of every one hundred. She knows that she is a traitor, and if she is caught she will be executed.

Hiding among the icy reeds, she fidgets with a lock of her hair. Across the Tumen lies the snowless landscape of the other country; her perception of distance is confused by the darkness. She snaps one of the reeds, melts its icy skin, and drinks the water. She does this over and over. Afterward, she breaks through the reeds and onto the Tumen; she falls into a long slide. Then somehow she manages to get back on her feet. Keeping her balance, she is running now. She hears no gunshots, only her labored breathing— the sound of her desperation. Suddenly the solidness of the river's surface is gone. A single step and she is in the air before hitting the ice cold waters. Her legs and arms thrash about in the rapids; the river is in her mouth and ears and nose and freezing her eyes. Pain bolts through her body.

The river leaves her on the bank—just past the Chinese town of Kaishantun.

THE TOWN is less than thirteen miles downriver, but I have seldom been there. From the moment my father first told me about the place I have despised it, despised the way that the town pollutes the Tumen with its factories. I know I am close to Kaishantun when I see first the town of Sambong across the river, which I know lies diagonally to it. I can already smell the chemicals and sulfur in the air.

I have packed enough food to last several days, but that does not dictate the length of my trip. Only the weather will decide. While I eat, I remove the binoculars from my backpack and focus them on a large white building. In front of the building, below the Kim Jong Il Sambong Station sign, a gathering of people attracts my attention. I observe seven or eight people who have formed a human pyramid. The man at the top loses his balance and the pyramid collapses in upon itself. They pick themselves up off the snow-covered ground and start again. The same man has made it back on top, and this time he maintains his balance. Someone below hands him a broom. He sets the broom on the first tier of the roof before boosting himself up. Twice the man slips while walking across the roof, but he has made it to the front wall of the second tier with the broom high above his head; he begins to sweep. The group of people, which has now grown, stands back from the entrance in order to see him sweeping. The broom slides back and forth, working its way lower. The man's arms are nearly straight out in front of him. Back and forth the broom goes, sweeping away the patina of snow, revealing the black hair, sweeping the black-rimmed glasses, sweeping the nose and smiling face. The same face that was on the badge I bought the girl.

After the break, each step seems more difficult. I lift my feet with great effort and continue until I come to the sharp bend in the river. Kaishantun. Perhaps this is the same view that she had seen.

I watch the brown sliver of river run through the stark frontier, trying to escape the season, flowing along, ignoring that the temperature is fifteen degrees below freezing.

Onto the river I step, forty yards from where it flows. It is smoothed and buffed by the wind, and I move with confidence. I approach the stretch of the Tumen that is unfrozen, and drop to my knees. Lying flat on my stomach, I slide the few feet to where the river runs unabated, remove my right glove, reach down, and touch the stunningly cold water and feel it swirling around my hand. The river gives me the answer that I seek: all she told me about herself, about the river not being completely frozen, was true. The factories in my country are working, and the heat from the pollution is enough to keep this side of the river flowing—only I hadn't thought of that. Although my hand has started to ache from the icy water, I find myself reaching deeper into it, and touching the edge of the ice to discover its thickness—where the river passes freely beneath it.

You become nothing more than a ghost, sleepwalking farther away from the city of Utopia. The river leaves you no choice but to cross.

But the freedom that awaits you is a prison of knowing that your daughter is somewhere back on the other side.

A mile from my farm the flurries have become coin-sized flakes and soon I know that the sky will be a solid white. I hurry as fast as I can but I am engulfed by the storm. Standing still, I struggle with my sense of direction and decide to drop to the ground, hoping it will give me a better perspective. I reach back and touch the snowshoes; I can't see them. I know I am in trouble. I must keep moving, but as I inch forward I feel a dull pain in my nose. I have hit something: a tree, the house, the shed? I grasp at the blizzard until my hand touches something solid. I move my hand along its length and, at last, I recognize it: my bench. The last time I lay on it, my head was pointing west and my feet east. Which end of the bench did I just hit with my nose? One is toward the border, the other is toward my house.

My mind is clumsy and begs me to stop and rest, plummet into sleep. I feel as if I am crawling uphill. I remember the warmth of my mother's hands covering my ears until they were warm. Deeper into the snow I burrow.

It is the smell of moldy smoke that stirs me. A familiar scent of a winter's house. But the weak odor of cold crushed corn makes me nauseous. I wait to see which part of my body I can move first. My mouth is so parched. I try to open my eyes but can't manage this. My eyelids are made of cast iron.

"Is there any water?" I drag out the words.

I am handed a pouch and I squeeze the water into my mouth. It is cold and refreshing.

"Thank you."

"It is from the river."

We are speaking the language of my father. My hand touches the floor and immediately I know it is my brick *kang*, I recognize the slight dip. The *kang* is cold.

Opening my eyes hurts like I have stumbled into a beehive.

"How long have I been here?"

"Blizzards erase all time. More than a day for certain."

"You found me?"

"We found one another."

"I don't remember."

"You were only steps away from your door."

I am sitting now and see the man at the opposite end of the stove wearing a pair of my thick-padded winter trousers and several of my cotton jackets.

"Why didn't you leave me out there?"

"Because you can help me."

"Why don't you just take what you want and go back to your country?"

"It is not only food that I want. I was the only one in the foxhole; my comrade went back to the barracks and must have been caught in the blizzard because he hadn't returned. I stayed alone for a long time and then decided to cross back over."

I manage to lift myself off the *kang* and go to the door. The lock has been destroyed; I open the door and look out.

The storm has gone and the sky is gray, the clouds race low and swift. I am able to stand straight although my body throbs.

"There was no way inside, so I shot the lock."

I think of the day when the soldiers came for the girl's body. Without his uniform he seems even smaller than the day he came looking for food.

"What have you done with your uniform?"

"I burned it in the stove when I came here."

I open the flu the entire way to allow the smoke to escape from the house.

"And your rifle?"

The soldier lifts and shows it to me.

"How long are you planning on staying?"

"Until the weather breaks."

"And what if they come looking for you?"

"Then we are both in trouble."

"I will move some blankets into the shed and give you some food. You can stay out there, not in here with me."

As I talk, I gather some straw and corn husks and place them under the *kang,* then light them; it will be warm tonight.

"Did you shoot the girl?" I surprise myself asking the question.

"No. My comrade did."

"There was more than one shot fired."

"I fired my rifle above her head."

I remember how there was only one bullet wound in the girl.

"Why would you kill a child?"

"I didn't kill her. I tried helping her when she came looking for food. I was the one who allowed her to cross. Last summer we were given orders to shoot anyone who tried crossing the river. No questions. Just shoot them. All of the traitors, coming to your country, are embarrassing the leadership."

"And now you are a traitor."

"When I entered the military we had to be of a certain height and weight, but now those requirements are disregarded. Last year, we started cultivating our own beans and we raised goats, but the winter killed the goats. Everything, even for the soldiers, has become too much in my country."

They are called ginseng artists, those who take a root and manipulate it, adding knobs and growth rings so that they may deceive the buyer into thinking it is an older, more valuable root. I have never met any of these artists, only heard about them. I can, however, imagine how they do it and can understand, but never justify, why.

Holding it up, I examine the great root; the severed beard lies on the table next to me. I have kept them wrapped in moist towels in order to preserve their natural state, and both pieces appear almost the way they were on the day the dirty-faced man startled me and I sliced them apart. The growth rings and knobs, the pearly spots on the beard, are all there, and with a magnifying glass I examine and match the rootlets of the beard. Each night, before the winds howl me to bed, I ponder how I might splice together the rootlets, making them whole again.

My only break from the root is when I take food out to the shed. The snow is shin to knee high, although it must be early March. I can't be certain of this since the firewood in the front room no longer serves as a gauge to the passage of time, now that it must keep two of us warm instead of one.

On the floor, the bearded soldier sleeps, undisturbed by my opening the door. He told me how he would sit in his foxhole and observe my daily life: my working in the cornfield, or weeding the garden, or leaving the house on my way to hunt, and returning. I know now that the soldiers knew much more about me than I ever did about them. The soldier's beard is unkempt. I think of bringing him a razor, but each time I return to the shed I forget.

After days of examining the rootlets, I wake at last with the understanding of how to fuse them together. Today I don't have the spirits of my father and uncle peering over my shoulder. I join the parts of the great root together and place it in some soil. Each day I sprinkle it with water.

When the weather breaks, I will take the great root to Yanji and try to sell it, and I will bring the soldier to the truck driver. Only after I have rid myself of the root and the soldier will I be able to forget this past year and start my life again.

Outside the winds have eased. I think I hear the dripping of ice and open the door. It is true; winter has begun its slow, slow melt. A little more every day. The nights, however, still halt and preserve the days' work of nature. That is how winter lets go of this valley, piece by piece, until the nights too are warm enough to help the days work their way toward spring.

THE NEW CENTURY'S FIRST SPRING

JUST AS it has done for thousands of springs, the river begins its thaw. There is little variation from year to year. The birds and mammals soon will return, as will the longer days and warmer weather. The valley still bears the vestiges of winter. Frozen fossils of squirrels and raccoons and pit vipers. The tips of icicles nearly meet the earth and drip into their self-created puddles; losing their grips, their glasslike spears shatter to the ground. Snow slides from the branches, flinging them back and forth before they settle. In time they will creak back to their natural positions, remaining there until the next frost.

The Tumen's melt begins unnoticed. Many weeks pass from the time when the Tumen starts its labored groans of thawing to the moment when the ice separates. The river takes so long to melt that the willows and birch and oaks by its banks will have already begun to blossom. But the pink camellias and the dogwood trees are more patient; they wait for the river's currents to come alive before they burst into bloom.

I AM always in such a rush to get back to my farm, but today I stay here in Yanji wasting time until I have no choice but to spend another night. I no longer care if the soldier is in my shed.

The great root is in my backpack where it has remained all day. I want to sell it, but I don't trust myself with any of my longtime buyers; it's not worth losing two generations of loyalty to my family.

I walk the streets looking for her: in the face of a waitress, a shop clerk, the woman lying on the bench in the train station. I am surprised with the trouble I have recalling her face, even a single feature. The hills of her spine, however, are etched clearly in my memory.

I sit on the far side of the lake; the low-lying sun slips in and out of the trees, casting shadows across my legs. People are peddling swan boats and a chill has captured the air. On the opposite side of the lake a shawl of lights is coming on, and I walk toward it. This area of Victory Park is illuminated by the colored lights of the Ferris wheel. The amusement rides are not, as I had thought, dead. When I gaze long enough at the Ferris wheel, all its lights blend together into threads of multiple colors, much like the different colors of paint that my uncle would mix together.

Different sounds come from different sections of the park: shrieks from those on the spinning rides, giggles from those whose figures are being distorted by the elongated mirrors. Did I ever hear her laugh? I tread lightly on this thought. The mottled figures in the mirrors captivate me: stubby, pointed heads, giraffe necks, scrunched legs. I like best the mirror that shrinks my legs and stretches my torso.

I recede to a dimmer area of the park and lean against a tree, placing the side of my face against its smooth bark. Without looking I know it is a birch, and I begin to feel steady enough to go forward, on my own.

A man sits at an easel, facing a young girl's twin on the parchment next to her. She doesn't move; the man sketches the shadows around her eyes, and those cast by her small nose. The picture is finished and the girl lets out a long-held smile, a smile of relief; she seems pleased with the drawing. He puts the drawing into a bag and hands it to her, the group of onlookers disperses, and I am alone with the artist.

"Do you want a drawing of yourself?"

"Yes."

I realize my mistake.

"No, not of myself, of a young girl I know. About the same age as the one you have just drawn."

"Do you have a photo of her?"

"A photo? No, I don't."

"Can you describe her to me?"

"She's about ten years old but looks much younger; sometimes, though, much older."

"How is her hair cut?"

"It is the straightest, blackest hair. Black and thick as a bear's."

"Is it long or short?"

"At the shoulder."

"How about her face?" the artist asks.

"Imagine the most glorious star. A star that allows you to forget the deepest of your troubles, allows you to breathe again."

The artist leaves the colored pencils in their tin, and all the while he is eyeing me, searching for what isn't there. Not so different from the way a ginseng hunter hunts.

"What else can you tell me about her?"

"What more is there to tell?" I reply, and leave the artist without a pencil in his hands.

I no longer go to Miss Wong's hotel. I have found another place, closer to the park. On this night, in the embrace of a woman, I pinch my eyes tight and imagine that the room isn't dank, that the walls aren't flecked with chips of paint, that the woman beside me isn't who she is, and, most of all, that I am not who I have become.

The next morning, I stop in front of the window of the same electronics store that mesmerized her. On the screen I see a man, wearing a matching gray jacket and pants, break away from the young woman whom he is with outside the half-open gate of the Japanese Consulate in the provincial capital of Shenyang. He takes a long stride, then another, toward the gate, and is almost running when the guard, in his green army uniform, reacts and lunges from his platform, grabbing the man's right shoulder. The asylum seeker, however, has momentum and surprise to his advantage, and he frees himself and runs through the opening of the gate and into the consulate's compound.

The scene is played over and over on the televisions and each time I see something new. A younger woman in a pink coat and black pants is carrying a large bundle on her back, and when the guards drag her away from the gate, the bundle falls; I see that it is a child, not more than five or six years old. The little girl is screaming, her pigtails are astray, the left one pointing to the sky, the right to the cement walkway of the compound. In the struggle with the guards, the woman claws and kicks, and the round-topped hat of one of the guards flies off and rolls by the girl, wobbling past the gate and into the compound. A diplomat picks up the hat, brushes it off and, once the gate has slammed shut behind him, hands the hat to a security guard. I watch the woman and girl being taken away by the police. All logic tells me that the woman isn't my lover, she looks nothing like her; but, I think, there is no logic in what we are permitting to happen.

On the same street, a couple of blocks from the electronics store, the old woman sits, leaning against a light pole, her meager goods spread on the ground at her bare feet: spoons, a knife, chopsticks, straggles of seaweed. There are no dogs with her today. She looks up. I am not sure whether she recognizes me, but it doesn't matter.

"How much is the seaweed?"

"Two *yuan*."

"I'll take it."

"All of it?"

I nod and reach into my jacket, take out the money that the truck driver gave me months ago for the two young men. It is the first time I have touched it since the exchange was made. I stuff the money into the crinkled hands of the woman. We look into each other's eyes, briefly but knowingly: a look that transcends rivers and cultures, no need for language.

"Do you have a name?"

"Soo," she answers without hesitation.

"You go home, Soo."

I carry the seaweed under my arm, never looking back, but knowing that she is folding each of the bills and will soon be swallowing them for her return journey across the river.

I bring the soldier a pan of hot water, a mirror, scissors, and a straight-edge blade.

"It is time for you to leave," I tell him. "I will take you in an hour."

"Where are we going?"

"I have to move you away from here. You told me yourself that the soldiers can easily see my farm from across the river, and most of what goes on here."

He is quiet and gives me a glance before turning away.

"I don't know what else to do. Maybe if things were

different here along the border, then you could stay. The farm is becoming more difficult for me to maintain. I could use the help."

I leave him alone and go back to the house. As I did for the two young men, I prepare some food for the soldier. I have a backpack, also with some food. After I take the soldier to the truck driver, I plan to go up into the mountain for the first time this year.

An hour after sunrise we leave, walking along the path behind the farm. The soldier has trimmed his beard, but has not shaven it off. He isn't even thirty years old; the beard makes him look older. I have told him to leave his rifle behind. After two miles, the soldier asks me to stop.

"I haven't eaten anything, and my legs are tired. Can we rest for a little while?"

"Only a short while. We are meeting a man who will soon be waiting for us."

We sit on tree stumps, twenty yards off the path. The soldier eats methodically, while I chew a piece of dried ginseng. The morning is clear and cool. Last night nearly reached a frost; such a struggle for this valley to rid itself of winter. Birds are out and flying from leafless tree to tree. I stand and stretch and the soldier looks up at me, finishing his final bite of cornbread.

"Other than in the capital city of Pyongyang, the best assignment for a soldier is on the frontier."

I have no response.

"In order to receive an assignment to the frontier, a soldier must prove his deep loyalty to the regime. I was serving in one of the reeducation camps and the duty was grinding. All the prisoners, traitors most of them, hundreds and hundreds of them, were filthy and the stench was horrible. It was almost unbearable and I had to get out of there. I knew that I had to do something unimaginable to catch the attention of my superior.

"One day in early spring, my chance came. I never planned anything like this; I knew that if I planned something so terrible I would never be able to go through with it. There were many children in this camp, some who had tried to escape, others who were caught stealing, others who were caught here in China. I was patrolling the huge grounds, making sure that no one stopped doing the work they were performing. There was a young boy, maybe eight, maybe twelve. The boy was working alongside a large pit filled with fetid water; he was hauling buckets of mud for making bricks. The boy had put down his bucket and was just standing there by the edge of the pit. I saw my superior look in my direction and I screamed at the boy, making sure that I still had my superior's attention. I went over to the boy and kicked him as hard as I could, right in the back. I may have even broken it, I'm not sure. The boy fell into the pit and didn't even try to fight or swim his way out. He just disappeared. The following week I was awarded the assignment to come here to the border. I had proven my loyalty."

I hold out a piece of dried ginseng and the soldier takes it. I realize that I have been standing the entire time the soldier has been talking. Again, I sit on the tree stump.

"Why didn't you do more to help the girl?"

"I tried to help her, but if my comrades saw me, I would have been executed for treason. She had nothing to offer us, so I couldn't be seen helping her."

"She was a child. What could she offer you?"

"Bribes. Food, perhaps. If we are given enough money or food, we allow the people to cross the river."

"And the girl had no money."

"That is why I told her to bring me half of whatever she brought back from your farm. I didn't think she would come back, I thought she would stay over here."

"She was afraid that you would come looking for her."

"When we shot her, I knew that I had to escape, I could no longer remain there."

"You told me you didn't shoot her."

"I didn't. At least it wasn't my bullet that killed her. But I did nothing to prevent it; I allowed it to happen. Maybe, if I had been the one who shot her, I wouldn't have had to come here. Killing a person is sometimes easier on the mind than not doing anything to prevent it."

Up through the trees I study the light, thinking that probably too much time has passed and the truck driver may have already left.

"We must move on."

The soldier rises.

"Are you still tired?"

"I will be okay. My legs are just weak from being inside for so long."

"The first week of the hunting season is also the most difficult for me."

The soldier follows and soon we come upon a path that

splits in several directions. I give him another piece of ginseng and then a third.

"Chew this while you are walking, it will give you energy. We have a long climb ahead of us."

I lead the way, the path is steep. My legs burn. After climbing two thousand feet, we stop. Both of us breathe heavily and it is a while before we recover enough to be able to speak. I wipe my brow and turn away from the soldier.

"Sometimes even spring isn't enough for a man to recover from winter."

He asks me where we are going.

"There is a place, high up in the mountains, where my father, many years ago, hid from the Japanese army. Both my father and grandfather are from your country. The forest is a good place to hide, and you will be safe up there until I decide what to do with you. I hunt ginseng up in that forest and I will bring you food, and maybe, someday, I will teach you how to hunt the root."

The soldier says nothing. I too have nothing more to add. We continue the climb, and before the sun reaches noon we have made it to the coniferous forest. I leave the soldier behind at the grandfather redwood and climb the remainder of the way alone.

To the treeless plateaus, the scrublands, the land of thorny shrubs and grounds of moss, to where rivers are born. Each spring I come here and find comfort in the forest frogs, knowing that when they hatch from their eggs, the hunting season is upon me. This has always been a place for me to remember, but today I come here to surrender myself to forgetting.

Now that I am alone, away from the soldier, her words are back with me again.

As a child, springtime had truly arrived when the pampas grass grew as high as my head and it had to be cut and burned in order to prevent a fire from starting in the dryness of summer. A single fire could burn the hillside and rush down and overtake the village. I never helped with the actual burning, but my mother and father did. I remember staying home on those days, and I had to keep the windows closed because the ash would be carried to the village and beyond.

My parents would return home from the hills, white triangles on their faces from where they wore wet towels, which protected them from the smoke and ash. One night each burning season my father would tie one of these towels around my face and take me up to the hills. I would wear a pair of his work boots, straw stuffed in the toes so that my feet would not slide. I would always be tired walking up the hills; maybe it was the awkwardness of the boots that made the climb more difficult than it really was. When we arrived amid the enormous ribbons of blackened grass, my father would hold my hand and we would run, kicking up the embers all around us. I used to imagine that the sparks were fireflies, squalls and squalls of them. My father said that for him they were the galaxy——they made him feel as if he were running through the universe itself.

There are times when I imagine her studying the map that I drew for her, and imagine—wherever she is—she is beginning her journey to my farm. There will be a soft knocking on my door and I will open it. She will be standing there; I will tell her to come in and warm herself on the *kang*.

Warm for late April. I am down by the river, standing on top of a small knoll overlooking it. I work a hoe into the rich, dark brown soil. For the past two days I have been down here readying the field for planting. Eggplant. Potatoes. Pumpkins. Sunflowers.

This garden is on the eastern side of my farm, visible from my house as well as from the opposite side of the river. I will prevent no one from eating from the garden; everyone will be welcome. Come autumn, if no one has eaten the food, I will then harvest and store it in the shed.

I need a rest and lean on the handle of the hoe. This garden is about the size of the one from my childhood in which I painted the ants. Weeks later when I was helping my mother weed the garden, out of the corner of my eye I spotted the blue ant and then the red one. I watched them move through the garden, one after the other, in the order I had painted them. Forty years later, the memory makes me smile.

I turn my attention to the river and imagine its journey past the city of Tumen, to where it takes an abrupt turn to the east and then south; from there it soon reaches its mouth, the murky waters merging with the azure blue sea, no longer carrying with it the burden of being a border.

I remove the hoe from the ground and return to my work. Only when the planting is completed will I take to the path up the mountain, and begin the hunting season anew.

Acknowledgments

I WOULD LIKE TO THANK all those nameless faces I met along the border and in the cities of Tumen and Yanji; this book is for all of you. Also to Duck-soo and Mun for the place to stay, for the ginseng, and for information on the ginseng hunters; to the individuals whose names I cannot put into print but whose information on life inside North Korea was invaluable; to Lorna Owen, my editor, for her faith in this book and for her tireless work to make it better; my publisher, Nan Talese; Bill Schierberl for his keen interest in this subject; all my friends back in Japan, thanks for the many years of memories; to Dean for the pens; and my wife, Aya, and son, Sam.